RISE OF THE FAE

DRAGON'S GIFT: THE DARK FAE BOOK 5

LINSEY HALL

For Ayse and Brett, my inspiring friends.

1

_____

THE LOVE OF MY LIFE SAT TIED TO A CHAIR, THRASHING against the bonds as his eyes glowed gold and black. I gripped my sister's hand and stared at him. My legs were so weak that I thought I might turn into a puddle at any moment.

"He's under her spell still," Aeri said. "It's been over an hour, and it hasn't faded."

I swallowed hard, nodding. Unable to speak.

An hour ago, we'd escaped the Unseelie kingdom. The land of the Dark Fae was ruled by my mother, the false queen, and she'd hit Tarron with something awful as we'd escaped through the portal back to earth. We'd brought him directly back to our workshop and bound him with unbreakable chains. The rest of our friends were recovering after the battle, but we had work to do.

Namely, curing Tarron.

"Whatever that spell was, it's infected his mind. The

false queen is particularly good with mind control." I stepped closer to him, and he growled, his eyes alight with hatred. We'd magically gagged him, but the growls were clear enough.

He'd been poisoned to hate me.

To want to kill me.

I dropped to my knees next to his chair and drew a knife from the ether. My heart thundered as I dragged the blade across my wrists.

"What are you doing?" Aeri demanded.

"The only thing I can." My voice broke. "Healing him."

"You don't even know if it's possible."

"I have to try." I was a Dragon Blood, for fates' sake. I could create any kind of magic I wanted.

More blood equaled more magic, and I wanted the biggest magic there was.

Pain flared as I dug the knife deeper, determined to pour out as much of my blood as I could.

Aeri fell to her knees at my side and gripped my arm. "Mari, slow down."

I looked at her, desperate. "I have to fix him, Aeri. I have to try."

Giving this much blood—all of it, really—would make the power permanent within me. It could also kill me.

Which Aeri knew.

It was always dangerous to make a new, permanent power.

My head grew light from blood loss and I swayed.

"Fine," Aeri snapped. She began to feed her magic into me, giving me strength.

Burn, the Thorn Wolf, appeared at my side, pressing his spiky body against my leg for support. I leaned into him despite the prickliness.

He and Aeri kept me upright as I poured my blood to the ground. It gleamed around me, black and bright. I gave my magic along with it, forcing it outside of myself. Darkness began to creep in at the edges of my vision.

I imagined the power I wanted—the ability to heal whatever ailed Tarron. *I can do this. I have to.*

I kept going, forcing my life and my magic out of me. My breathing quickened and my skin grew cold. Blindness stole over me.

"It's too much." Aeri's voice filtered in as if from a distance.

I swayed, nearly toppling over. Fear pierced me.

If this didn't work—if the magic didn't turn—I would die.

Then it snapped in the air. The magic changed, growing to suit my visions. The power surged back into me, and I gasped. Strength filled my muscles, and magic sparked through my soul.

My eyes popped open, and I could see, clearer and sharper than ever. The air felt fresh. And I felt powerful.

I stood, pushing away from Aeri and Burn.

Tarron stared at me, hatred and rage in his eyes.

It's not him.

Shaking, I pressed a hand to his shoulder. My new

magic raged inside of me, the healing power bursting to break free. I fed it into him, watching with delight as the cut on his brow healed.

It's working.

I gave it everything I had, pouring as much healing energy as I could into him. I would force away the false queen's influence, drive away the curse that twisted his mind. Heal him.

It took everything I had, though. He soaked up my magic like a sponge, but never stopped growling at me.

Weak, I went to my knees. He thrashed, trying to get away. I kept going.

"Mari, stop." Aeri grabbed my arm. "It's not working."

I didn't stop. She yanked at me, and I was too weak to fight her.

Gasping, I sat back.

Tarron glared at me, his lips forcibly shut by our magical gag.

Tears pricked at my eyes. "It didn't work."

"We'll find an antidote." Aeri pulled me to my feet.

"I tried, and I'm not strong enough. I don't have what it takes." I would never be as strong as the false queen. Never be able to undo her curse on Tarron *or* stop her from destroying our kingdoms.

"Get it together." Aeri shook me, her eyes intense. "This isn't you. Come on, now."

I gasped, blinking back tears.

She was right.

I staggered backward, staring at Tarron.

This was rock bottom.

I drew in a shuddery breath. "We need a plan."

"Let's figure out what the curse is exactly," Aeri said. "Then we can find the right antidote."

I nodded. Just because I couldn't heal him didn't mean there wasn't a solution. "Yeah. We'll heal Tarron. Then, I'm going to find a way to become stronger so that I stop that bitch from ever doing anything like this again."

I wasn't strong enough now, but I would be.

Aeri squeezed my shoulder. "Come on."

I sucked in a deep breath and went to the shelf full of my blood sorcery supplies. We had a spell for this. It wasn't super precise, but it would give us a clue about what was wrong with him. I'd hoped I could hit him with such a huge healing blast that I'd drive out whatever curse there was, but apparently we needed to do this the hard way.

Quickly, I gathered the tiny bottles of ingredients. Aeri collected the onyx bowl and silver dagger. I retrieved the pink crystal that came from a realm not on earth, and we got to work mixing the potion that would reveal the nature of Tarron's curse.

She carefully measured out the ingredients, and I dropped the crystal in. Slowly, I stirred the mixture with the silver blade.

"We'll fix him, Mari. Don't worry."

My throat tightened. Tarron and I had *just* confessed our love for each other. And then *this*. He'd thrown himself in front of the curse to save me.

In the chair, he thrashed.

"We'll fix you, I promise," I said.

He just growled.

Tarron was gone. In his place was a creature I didn't recognize. It wore the face and body of my beloved, but it wasn't Tarron.

Burn prowled toward him, big head low and eyes flaming as he watched the Seelie king. The Thorn Wolf positioned himself between us, and I turned my back to Tarron. I couldn't bear to see him like this.

Carefully, I added the ingredients to the bowl. The hearth flickered with warmth and light, but it did nothing to drive away the coldness in my soul.

When all the ingredients had been added, Aeri raised the silver dagger. "Ready?"

I nodded.

She sliced her fingertip, wincing slightly, and let the white blood drip into the bowl.

I took the glinting blade from her and did the same, feeling the pinch of pain as it bit into my flesh. We only used this blade when the spell was extra important—and this definitely qualified.

I shook my finger so a few drops of black blood dripped into the potion. The mixtures sizzled. Quickly, I stirred the potion with the blade, watching as the black and white blood mixed with the purple liquid.

"Do you want me to get his blood?" Aeri asked.

"I'll do it." I took the knife and bowl to Tarron, who fought even harder against the bonds. Briefly, I glanced at his face, then away.

"This won't hurt much." I knelt behind him, moving toward the spot where his hands were bound behind him.

Gently, I sliced his fingertip and let the red blood drip into the bowl. The dagger was imbued with magic that would make the cut heal quickly.

I rose silently.

Tarron snarled as I walked back toward my sister.

My heart pinched. Even though I knew it was the false queen's magic at work, it still stung.

"Get a move on," Aeri said. "Quicker we do this, quicker he's better."

I nodded and looked away from him, hurrying toward the table. Together, Aeri and I leaned over the bowl. Burn joined me, pressing his thorny side against my leg. I scratched his neck, grateful for the moral support.

Aeri and I stared down into the bowl. Tarron's blood mixed with the potion, and I gave it another stir with the silver blade.

I held my breath, waiting. It would turn different colors depending upon the nature of his curse.

The potion turned blue—a faint periwinkle that would be pretty if it weren't for the message it sent.

"The soul." I blinked, then looked at Aeri. "That's strange."

"I would have thought it affected his mind, not his soul."

"It must be some mutated version of the false queen's power."

The potion turned black.

My stomach pitched and my skin chilled. "Death."

The black transitioned to silvery blue almost immediately.

"What the hell?" Aeri said. "That's never happened before. It always ends on black."

I frowned. "I don't understand. Normally the potion turning black indicates that the curse will kill you."

"Perhaps it will kill his soul," Aeri said.

I drew in an unsteady breath. "That's not better."

"There was no mention of his mind. If the curse controlled his mind, the potion would have turned green."

"It controls his soul." I shuddered. This was far worse than what she'd done to me. She'd tried to control my mind with her cursed power, but I'd been able to fight it. "He can't resist it because she's got her hooks into his soul.

"Maybe that's why your new healing power didn't work on him," Aeri said.

I shook my head. "It should have. I think I'm just not strong enough."

"You can do anything."

"Anything except defeat the false queen, it seems." I shook my head. I needed to become as strong as her. To gain her skills so I could take her out and protect everyone I loved.

Finally, the potion faded to gray. It was done.

Aeri put on a determined face. "Let's consult the book."

I nodded, my mind on autopilot. The potion had revealed the fundamental nature of the curse—but to find the specific curse itself, we'd need more information.

I strode to the bookshelf on shaking legs, taking down a massive leather-bound tome. *Curses Most Deadly and Rare* was one of our most useful books.

I flipped through the pages, skimming quickly for any mention of a soul curse that would lead to a fate worse than death.

Finally, I found something.

The Ataraxia Curse -- Mind Control Through the Soul.

Aeri jabbed the words with her finger. "That's it."

Breath held, I skimmed the text. "It says that only one who already possesses the power of mind control can wield this curse."

"Just like the false queen."

"Except she enhanced her magic and turned it into soul power. Now she can control her victim without being near them. It's so much more powerful than what she tried to do with me."

"He is already her minion."

I glanced toward Tarron, who fought against the bonds. His powerful muscles strained, and he growled low in his throat when he caught sight of me watching him.

Minion would never be a good descriptor for him, but he was definitely under the false queen's sway.

"What does it say for a cure?" I turned back to the book and scanned.

"There is no cure." Aeri's tone darkened.

"There has to be. Just because it doesn't say so here, doesn't mean there isn't one." I reached the bottom of the page. It provided only the tiniest bit of hope. "It says there is a potion that can dampen the effects."

"But it won't eliminate her influence. He'll still be slowly losing his soul."

"But it will buy us time." Desperation surged through me.

"A few days at most."

I shot her a glare. "I'll take them." My mind raced. "If we can hold off the effects and kill the false queen, her curse will break."

"Will it?" Aeri asked. "Or will it take him with her, if their souls are bound."

"Shit." That was the more likely outcome.

She squeezed my hand. "We *will* find a way around this."

I swallowed hard and gripped her hand tightly, focusing on her words.

"First step's first." She bent over the ingredient list for the potion that would dampen the effects of the spell. "It looks like we have everything we need except for the root of Paeoria."

"That's traditionally a Fae ingredient." I frowned. "I wonder if they have it in their realm?"

"He has a comms charm, doesn't he?"

I nodded, then strode toward him. He thrashed against the bindings, growling at me. Thank fates for the gag—I didn't want to hear whatever he'd say to me right now.

I skirted around him, avoiding looking at his face, and

knelt at his back. Quickly, I removed the comms charm tied around his wrist.

Unlike a cell phone, it could only contact one person—but the line was always open. As long as you weren't dead.

I raised it to my lips. "Luna? Are you there?"

"Mari, is that you?" Tarron's second-in-command sounded perplexed.

"It is."

"What's happened to Tarron? I had to leave the forest earlier, and he hasn't returned to the Seelie Court. Nor have I heard from him."

"He's..." I glanced down at him. "Indisposed. Taking a shower."

Luna was loyal to him—I was nearly sure of it. All the same, I didn't want to tell his subjects that he was out of commission, held sway to an evil bitch who would make him kill me and all the Seelie if he could get free of his bindings.

"When is he coming back?" she asked.

"Soon. We're working on a plan to take out the false queen of the Unseelie."

"We want in," Luna said. "The whole royal guard."

"Thank you." We'd need all the help we could get, and the Seelie were the perfect people for it. After the false queen had burned much of their city and tried to murder them all, they were out for blood.

"What can I do for you now, though? Clearly you're calling about something important." Suspicion sounded in her voice, and I couldn't blame her. Rarely did someone allow another to use their comms charm.

"We need some root of Paeoria. I know that is commonly used in Fae spells."

"It is. But why do you need it?"

"For an antidote for my sister. She's unwell."

I shot Aeri a glance. She drew a finger across her throat, tilted her head, and stuck out her tongue.

"Oh no." Concern echoed in Luna's voice. "Aerdeca is sick?"

"Yes. Do you have the ingredient?"

"Let me check with our potions master. Give me a moment."

I waited, breath held, foot tapping.

By the time she returned, I was vibrating with anticipation. We *needed* this.

"I'm afraid we don't have it," Luna said. "But there's a guy in Glasgow. A Fae without a court. He runs a bar as a front, but his main business is Fae potion making."

Fae without a court were often dangerous. The Fae were a social people, often liking to stick to their groups. They were as pack-like as the shifters, but in a different way. When they went off on their own, they were often unstable.

"What's the bar called?" I asked. "And where in Glasgow, exactly?"

"It's the Whispering Rowan, located just off Union Street on the north end, down a flight of stairs that can be found in an alley marked with a stone rowan branch."

"So Fae," I muttered.

"We do love our trees." Her voice sobered. "But seriously, Mari. You need to be careful. He could be unstable."

"We will be. Promise."

"What's his name?"

"Kevin."

"Kevin?" I frowned. "That's not very Fae."

"I told you—he is a Fae without a court. He's taken a human name. But if you really want to get one over on him, call him Penriel."

"Penriel."

"Yep. Good luck. And tell the king that we await his command."

"I will."

She disconnected, and I couldn't help but feel that she didn't buy my story about Tarron.

"At least she didn't ask questions," Aeri said.

"Seriously. Is Declan done getting cleaned up, do you think? Could he keep an eye on Tarron while we're gone?"

Tarron had been hit by this curse while we'd been trying to rescue Aeri and her boyfriend. She'd gotten cleaned up first, getting into a fresh ghost suit so she was fight-ready, and he should be done in the shower any minute now.

"I'll check." She shot me a serious look. "But you need to eat something before we go. You look ready to drop."

I nodded, my stomach grumbling at the thought. Though food held little appeal, I needed to keep my strength up.

I looked at the Thorn Wolf. "Keep an eye on him, will you, buddy?"

He woofed low, then sat in front of Tarron, his eyes glued to the bound man.

Aeri went to find Declan while I hurried to my kitchen. Quickly, I put some bacon in the microwave—not ideal, but I wasn't rolling in time—then went to my bedroom and changed into fresh clothes. Fight wear, of course.

I grabbed a huge stack of cash from the bottom dresser drawer, just in case the root of Paeoria was pricey, and withdrew my potion bag from the ether. I stashed the cash in it and shoved the bag back into the ether.

By the time I made it into the kitchen, the microwave was beeping. I pulled out the hot plate and threw together two sandwiches.

I bit down into the first sandwich, and deliciousness exploded on my tongue. Life was always better with bacon. I ate as I returned to the workshop and handed Burn the second sandwich.

"For you, buddy. You earned it."

He nipped it gracefully out of my hand and chomped down.

Tarron had slumped in his bindings, finally exhausted from fighting against the enchanted metal.

"I'll keep an eye on him." Declan's voice sounded from behind, and I turned.

The fallen angel had wet hair from his recent shower, and Aeri stood at his side.

"Thanks. I don't think he can get out of those chains, but I'd hate to lose him if it happened."

Declan nodded.

Aeri approached. "Let's get a move on."

I held out my hand for her. She reached out and gripped my palm. I called upon my magic, envisioning St Vincent Street in Glasgow, with its wide road and massive stone buildings.

The ether sucked us in and spun us through space, finally spitting us out on the dark road in the middle of the city. Streetlights shed a golden glow on the creamy flagstone, and drunken revelers stumbled along ahead of us.

"It's got to be near midnight here," Aeri said. "The Fae pub will still be open."

"Good. We can pretend to be patrons." I spun in a circle to get my bearings, then pointed. "This way."

Together, we hurried down the street, headed toward the east end and the alley marked with the rowan bough.

As we walked, Aeri broke the silence. "So, if you overthrow your mother, that will make you queen, you know."

I swallowed hard. "Yep."

"You don't sound that excited about it."

"I haven't had a lot of time to think about it."

"Now that you have?"

The words blurted out of me. "I don't think I want it."

"The responsibility, you mean?"

"Exactly. The crown is fine, the deference and being called Your Highness—that all sounds great. Plus, the palace is fabulous. But it's so much work. So much responsibility. And it all takes place in another realm."

"And I thought *I* was gone from home a lot these days. You'd never be around."

"Exactly. We've built an awesome life in Magic's Bend. I like that life. I don't suddenly want to be doing a lot of bureaucracy—because that's what it is, if you're a decent queen. The boring minutia and stress of making sure everyone is okay."

Aeri shuddered. "Yeah, no thanks."

"It's definitely not how our mother is ruling." My heart twisted. "I can't believe that the only family I've ever known sucks. Our aunt. My mother."

"I don't suck."

I wrapped my arm around her neck and leaned my head against hers. "That, you do not."

"But I get it. Would be nice to have some good family besides the two of us."

I nodded, then shoved the thought away.

We passed several bars and restaurants before I spotted the stone rowan bough. It was subtle, but unmistakable. Compared to the other spots on the street, the Fae pub was distinctly lower key. A narrow set of stairs led down into the shadowed alley.

"There's not even a sign," Aeri said.

I glanced up at the rowan bough. "Just that thing, if you know to look for it."

"Do you think they'll let me in, since I don't have Fae blood?"

"Let's try."

She nodded and started down the stairs. I followed, keeping my footsteps silent on the stone. By the time we reached the bottom, the light from the street lamps above had faded. Faerie lights glittered a few feet over my head, shining a faint glow on the alley.

A narrow door stood at the end of the passage, closed tightly against the night air.

"Not very welcoming," Aeri muttered.

I frowned and strode up to it. "There's no door handle."

"But there is a little hatch." Aeri pointed to a tiny hatch set into the door, just above our eye level. "Should we knock?"

"What if there is a fancy knock we have to do and we screw it up and they know we're not regulars? Or invited?"

"Good point." She frowned, then pointed to the middle of the door. "Is that stain what I think it is?"

I peered at it, then nodded. "Definitely blood."

"Then you know what to do, fairy lady."

I smirked at her, then sliced my fingertip and pressed the bloody tip to the door, trying not to think about how gross it was.

Nothing happened.

I glanced at Aeri. "You try."

She shrugged and cut her finger, then pressed it to the door.

The little hatch on the door slid open, and she yanked her hand back. My gaze flew up to the hatch, meeting a pair of black eyes.

"What do you want?"

"A drink." Aeri glared. "I suggest you let us in if you don't wish to face our wrath."

I let loose with a bit of my magical signature, and Aeri did the same. It was the supernatural version of flexing your muscles, and it worked.

The eyes darted left and right, then the door creaked and swung open.

Aeri and I shared a glance.

Well, that had worked. And apparently Penriel wasn't a fan of the Fae, since her blood had worked and mine had not.

I stepped toward the door. The scent of the forest and a rushing river flowed out. Despite the welcoming sounds, the corridor within was dark and creepy.

"Definite creep vibes," Aeri muttered.

"Perfect," I said wryly. "Penriel is a weirdo."

2

I STEPPED INTO THE DARKENED CORRIDOR, DODGING TO avoid the hulking guard. Aeri followed.

A narrow stream burbled by on the right, rushing over rocks and flowing into a gap in the floor near the door. Tree branches arced overhead, full of black birds that stared down with red eyes.

"Don't move too fast or they'll attack," the guard grumbled. He wore a dark uniform that allowed him to blend into the corridor easily.

"Noted." I eyed them warily, determined not to incite their ire.

The bird closest to me cocked its head and cawed. I smiled, reaching up slowly to let it sniff at my fingers.

Could birds even smell?

The little creature pecked at my fingertips, clearly curious.

"Be careful..." the guard rumbled.

I wasn't sure what I was doing exactly, but we needed these birds to like us. If things went south in here and we had to make a run for it, I didn't want these cute little bastards pecking at my eyes.

"Hang on, buddy." I reached into my pocket and withdrew a few of the butterscotch candies I always kept on hand. I raised the handful to the bird, who took one.

Satisfied, the bird hopped to the side and chirped at me.

A few others came over and took the rest of the sweets.

"Thanks, guys." I strode under his branch, gratified that he didn't shit on me. "There's more where that came from."

The corridor ahead was long and narrow, forcing us into single file. The little river to my right widened as we neared the main entrance of the bar, splitting to enter the larger room and flow around the edges. A small bridge arced over it, and I strode across.

Aeri joined me on the bridge, which was wide enough for two, and we entered the dark underground bar side by side. The space was filled with comfortable chairs upholstered in green velvet. The river circled the entire space, filling the room with the scent of fresh water.

"This is nice. Places like this normally reek of booze," I muttered.

"And vomit," Aeri said. "But not for the Fae, apparently."

"Even their underground dive bars are fancy."

Trees were scattered throughout the space, dotted

between the chairs and couches and reaching over them with their limbs. It gave the feel of being in an underground forest. Faerie lights sparkled against the ceiling, coalescing in greater numbers near the long bar at the back. It appeared to be made of one massive tree trunk that had been smoothed off at the top.

The bartender looked human. I frowned.

"Weird," Aeri said. "I expected a Fae. Don't they tend to stick together?"

"They do, but Penriel is without a court."

Aeri shrugged. "Makes sense, then, I guess."

A few faces turned to watch us approach the bar. Most people sat in the comfy green chairs, chatting in quiet voices over drinks that gleamed golden.

"Shifter, witch, vampire, and demon," I murmured to Aeri, taking stock of the clientele. "Not a single Fae."

"Maybe I should do the talking, then," Aeri said. "Since he doesn't like your kind."

"Good plan." I'd never thought of myself as being particularly Fae-looking, but better safe than sorry.

We stopped in front of the bar.

The guy behind it looked up, a bottle of Buckfast in his hand. I grimaced at the sight of the fortified, caffeinated wine.

"What can I get you?" he asked.

"Two glasses of wine, please," Aeri said.

We rarely drank wine—preferring Manhattans and martinis—but at least it was low alcohol.

He raised the bottle of Buckfast. "This will do?"

"Not exactly what I was thinking," Aeri said.

I grimaced. Buckfast was made at an abbey in England near where Claire had been born. She'd brought us a bottle of the awful stuff once, and I'd vowed to never drink it again.

"How about a white." Aeri gave him her best smile.

"Suit yourself." He shrugged and turned back to the shelves of liquor.

I leaned against the bar, turning to inspect the room around us. The other patrons had turned back to their conversations, leaving us in a dark little bubble. On the left wall, I spotted a small dark door.

I called upon my Seeker sense, asking it to find Penriel. As I'd expected, it tugged hard toward the door.

Subtly, I pointed to it. "That leads to Penriel."

"I'll take care of this guy," Aeri murmured.

He returned with our glasses and set them on the counter. I caught sight of Aeri slicing her index finger with her sharp thumbnail.

"Thanks, handsome," she purred, leaning over the bar to get closer to him.

He leaned toward her, the grin already spreading across his face.

"So, you're not from around here?" he asked, his Glaswegian accent thick.

"What gave it away?"

"Well, your accent, for—"

Before he could finish the sentence, she swiped out and smeared a bit of her white blood over his forehead.

Her magic flared briefly, and her voice filled with suggestive power. "Take us though the black door."

He blinked, his eyes going unfocused.

I frowned.

The bartender stood stock-still, seeming dumbstruck. Or frozen.

Aeri leaned back. "Well, shit."

"You broke him." His eyes looked hazy and strange.

Gently, Aeri poked him in the chest. He didn't so much as move. "Damn it. I didn't see that coming."

"Neither did I. It never happens." I looked around to inspect the clientele. No one had turned to look at us. "Can you make a distraction so I can slip through the door?"

She nodded. "No problem. I'll meet you in there."

Silently, she snuck away, heading toward the ladies' room. A few heads turned to check her out, but she ignored them, going through the wooden door. A moment later, the door cracked open, though no one exited.

Aeri.

She'd used her ghost suit to become invisible. A few seconds later, the chair closest to the bathroom levitated into the air, then smashed down.

Every head—except the bartender's, which was weirdly frozen—turned in shock. Another chair went flying.

I grinned.

Aeri had the distraction under control, so I slipped toward the unguarded door. When I reached it, I grabbed the handle and tried to pull it open.

Nothing.

It was stuck solid.

Damn it.

I pulled harder, giving it some of my Dragon Blood strength, and the wood around the lock splintered. The door swung open.

Good enough.

I stepped into the dark little corridor. Here, there was no rushing river. Instead, fiery crystals were set into the wall, each seeming to contain an individual flame.

Quickly, I strode down the hall and into a large room. Four large tables sat in the space, each piled high with tiny jars and potion-making materials. There didn't seem to be any sort of organization, and I assumed Penriel was a bit of a mess.

The dirt walls of the space were threaded through with tree roots, and faerie lights glittered in the crevices.

Penriel might have forsaken any Fae courts, but there was no denying his Fae nature.

"Penriel?" I called out.

"Kevin," a voice snapped from the shadows. A slender man stepped out, his golden hair bright in the dimness of the room. "My name is Kevin."

Oookay. "Great. Kevin it is, then."

There had to be a reason he'd picked a super normal human name, and I didn't want to piss him off—yet. So I'd play it his way.

"How did you get back here?" he demanded.

"I have my ways."

"I don't like the sound of that." He tugged at his dark

shirt. Like most potion-masters, he seemed to favor all black. It was just practical. "Why are you here?"

"I need some root of Paeoria, and I heard you were just the guy."

His frown deepened. "That's rare. And expensive."

"Do you have it?"

"Maybe."

I sighed. "I'll pay, obviously."

"How well?"

Another presence appeared—invisible but unmistakable. Aeri had joined me. She stayed invisible, which was only smart.

I kept my eyes on Penriel instead of searching for her. "What do you want?"

"Ten grand."

Ouch. "That's pretty steep."

"And you're pretty desperate." He sneered, and it changed his whole face. He went from blandly handsome to rat-like in the flash of an eye.

"I'm not." I was proud of how stable my voice sounded.

"You are. I can see it on you." He tapped the side of his nose. "Fae power."

"Ten thousand, then. Fine. I just want to get out of here." I reached into the ether and withdrew my potion bag. Quickly, I yanked out wads of cash. It was bound in stacks of hundreds, and I made sure he didn't see that I had more than he'd asked for.

He gestured for me to approach. "Come on, then."

Was he being oddly twitchy?

Wary, I approached. "The root of Paeoria?"

"Money first."

"At the same time."

"Money first." His demand was antsy. Like an addict looking for a fix. Or an awkward weirdo trying to pull a fast one.

"Fine." I handed him the cash.

He grabbed it from me.

"The root of Paeoria?" I asked.

"It's time for you to go." He thrust out his hands, and magic exploded from his palms. I flew backward, an invisible force pushing me toward the door.

Panic flared. I struggled against his power, but was unable to break it.

Aeri.

He still didn't know she was here. Perhaps she could sneak through and take what we were after.

"And your invisible friend, too," he hissed.

Damn it.

Aeri shouted from my left, surprise in the sound. She appeared a half second later, scowling as she was forced back toward the door.

I considered throwing the Aranthian Crystal at him to freeze his magic, but hesitated.

No.

We'd worked hard to get that crystal from the Dark Necromancer. It hadn't worked against the false queen—not for long, at least—but we might still need it.

Quickly, I sliced my finger and smiled at the pinch of pain. I needed just a bit of magic...

I envisioned stopping time around Penriel, freezing him so his magic ceased and we could do what needed doing.

The magic surged in my veins as my Dragon Blood roared. It created new power, giving me a heady sense of strength.

Penriel froze solid, his face twisted in a sneer of victory.

The power that pushed me toward the door stopped abruptly, and I grinned.

Aeri stopped drifting backward and smiled, shaking her limbs out. "Good work."

"Doesn't work on strong supernaturals, but he's fairly weak." I brushed my hands off and stepped forward, staring at Penriel. "Your guards seemed to realize they were dealing with someone they shouldn't mess with. Shame you didn't get the memo."

I walked past him, calling upon my Seeker sense to find the root of Paeoria. "I sure hope this bastard has what we're looking for."

"The book said it would be withered and purple."

I searched fast, not wanting any of the bar patrons or guards to figure out what was going on. Soon enough they'd notice that the bartender wasn't moving.

Aeri and I searched the entire workshop and the little room beyond. The tiny space at the back was filled with potions and ingredients from floor to ceiling.

"A real treasure trove." I wished there were less of it though. The longer I searched, the more stressed I got.

Tarron needed me to find this ingredient, damn it.

Finally, I spotted a withered purple root in a little glass jar.

Root of Paeoria was scribbled on a tiny label.

"Bingo." I grabbed it and shoved it into my potion bag, then stashed the bag back in the ether. "Let's get the hell out of here."

I tried my transport power, but it didn't work. "Damn it, I'm blocked."

"Let's run for it."

Together, we hurried out of Penriel's workshop. As I passed him, I yanked the ten grand out of his hand. "I'd have let you keep it if you'd played fair."

"Jerk," Aeri hissed.

We left the workshop and hurried down the hall. As we reached the entrance to the main part of the bar, I caught the sound of a commotion.

"They're onto us," I whispered.

Shouts sounded on the other side of the door.

"Definitely."

"Use your invisibility." I reached into the ether and withdrew the little glass vial holding the root of Paeoria. I shoved it into her hand. "Get the hell out of here."

"I'm not leaving you."

"You *have* to. We need to save Tarron."

"Not at the expense of you."

"I'll be fine. Delayed maybe, but fine." I gripped her arm. "*Please.* I'd do it for you."

"Leave me behind?" She arched a brow.

"You know what I mean." I shoved her. "Now go."

She glared at me and took the root. "Fine, but I'm coming back for you as soon as I get this ingredient to Magic's Bend."

"Fine, whatever. Just go."

She nodded, then flipped up the hood on her white suit and disappeared.

The door in front of me creaked open as she slipped out, and I followed, determined to distract them from Aeri.

There had to be at least a dozen patrons and six guards, all scattered throughout the room, standing amongst the trees that grew up from the floor.

Now they were all looking at me.

"Intruder!" shouted one of the guards. He pointed to me, brow furrowed.

"Hey there!" I grinned and waved, then called upon my wings.

The ceiling wasn't high, but the tree branches provided cover. The guards began to hurl blasts of white magic at me. I darted and dived, narrowly avoiding the blows. A blast of white light hit a tree to my left, and the thing shuddered and dropped its leaves.

"Bitch!" shouted one of the guards.

I hissed but didn't attack. They were just doing their jobs. Running seemed fairest and safest.

I flew toward the door, racing for freedom.

A blast of green light hit my arm, and pain flared. I screamed, clutching my bicep as it went numb. Shocked, I looked behind me.

One of the patrons, a guy with a skinny black mustache and a long ponytail, grinned evilly at me.

He was just attacking for the hell of it!

Bastard.

I drew a potion bomb from the ether—a stunner, just to be nice—and chucked it at him. The glass exploded against his chest, tiny shards of blue glass flying through the air. The liquid soaked into his shirt, and he toppled backward, his eyes rolling back in his head.

Two guards sent massive blasts of white light at me, and I managed to narrowly avoid them, darting hard to the right and taking cover behind some tree limbs.

The branches shook, dropping their leaves.

I spun to face the door. *Nearly there.*

The corridor with the birds was so close.

Panting, I gave it one last burst of speed, my wings beating fast, and dived low through the doorway that led into the corridor. Guards shouted and sprinted after me.

"Hey, birdies!" I called, trying to sound as friendly as possible.

They started up a racket, turning dozens of pairs of beady red eyes on me. They snapped their black beaks and shifted restlessly, leaning toward me.

"Get her!" shouted one of the guards. "Go on, you useless birds!"

My heart pounded as I dug into my pocket and yanked

out a small handful of the gold-wrapped butterscotch candies. I chucked them in the air ahead of me. "For my buddies!"

The birds all gave a loud caw of delight and lunged off their branches, flying toward the golden candies. I darted past them, covering my face as I flew through the hordes of birds going the other direction.

"Don't forget to share!" I shouted as I raced toward the exit.

One last guard stood in front of it, braced for battle with his sword raised high.

There was no time to hunt for a stunning potion. I drew my blade from the ether and landed in front of him.

His blade was twice as long as mine. He swung it hard and fast for my abdomen, and I jumped backward, sucking in my stomach as the steel whooshed past.

"That was close." I grinned and sliced out with my own blade, going for his sword arm.

He tried to parry, but was too slow. My steel cut deep, slicing a wound that made him howl. He clutched the injury and staggered. I charged and kicked him in the gut, sending him to the ground.

Fast as I could, I leapt over him and shoved at the door, racing out into the cold night air. I sprinted through the alley and up the stairs, appearing on the wide flagstone street. Somewhere else in the city, bagpipes were playing, their plaintive wails sounding high above the majestic stone buildings.

"Good to see you again, Scotland." With that, I called

upon my transport magic and disappeared. The last thing I heard was the frustrated roar of Penriel, the Fae without a court.

I appeared back on the street in front of my house. Darklane was quiet at this time of day. Late afternoon was often one of the less busy periods, and there was no one on the street as I raced up the stairs to my townhouse.

As I disengaged the security charms that protected the front door, a roar sounded from within.

No.

Tarron.

I raced inside and down the hall, hurtling into the workshop at the back.

Tarron had somehow escaped his bindings and had Aeri cornered. He was about seven feet from her, backing her up against the wall. She swung her mace, her brow creased and a debate in her eyes.

My heart thundered.

Shit. They would kill each other.

3

TARRON ROARED AND CHARGED AERI, HIS EYES GOLDEN AND wild. Black veins shot through the glowing irises, evidence of the false queen's control. He was so enraged that he didn't even see me standing to the side.

Quickly, I reached into the ether and fumbled for a stunning charm in the bag.

Crap, I couldn't find one!

It took me far too long, but finally, my sweating fingers closed around the familiar shape. I withdrew it, heart thundering as I threw it at him, praying that my aim was true.

The blue glass globe spun through the air and slammed into his back, soaking his shirt with the solution. He flew forward and crashed onto his front, unconscious.

"Where is Declan?" I demanded as I hurried toward Tarron. "You shouldn't have been alone!"

"He's getting Connor. He wasn't picking up the phone. Anyway, I could handle him." She glared at me.

"But the mace, Aeri? You could have crushed his skull."

"I was just trying to scare him."

I laughed as I knelt at his side. "Scare Tarron?"

"Good point." She nudged him with her toe. "Big bastard doesn't look like he's scared of anything."

"Hey, that's the man I love you're talking about."

She met my gaze. "Love?"

"Yeah." I shrugged. "Apparently so." I swept the hair back from the side of his face, pleased to see that he hadn't landed straight on it. "Though he's clearly not at his best right now."

"No kidding." She crouched by his side. "So you really love him? It's not just the fated mates thing?"

"This wasn't really where I expected to have this heart to heart."

"What, you imagined more of a martini and Manhattan situation? Maybe while watching some *True Blood* and eating ice cream?"

"Well, yeah." I rolled Tarron over and felt his ribs, trying to make sure nothing was broken. He was unconscious, but he might still wince if I pressed a particularly sore spot. "But then again, none of this is what I expected."

"You're preaching to the choir here." She reached over and gripped my hand. "You're *sure* it's love?"

"What's not to love?" I gestured to him. "If you ignore this temporary insanity, he's kind, smart, funny, strong. Handsome, too. And he loves me back."

That was the big thing. I didn't think I would be able to handle unrequited love so well. I'd do it for Tarron—I wouldn't have a choice—but I was damned glad that the sane version of Tarron loved me back.

"He might not survive this," Aeri said, her tone soft.

I hissed at her. "He will."

She frowned, worry and sadness in her eyes. "I'm only saying that because I love you, Mari. You know this curse is a big one. We don't even know how to cure it yet. Or *if* it can be cured."

"It can be. It *has* to be." I drew in a deep breath. "Now where is Connor? He needs to make that antidote so that Tarron can have a bit of sanity while we look for the true cure."

Aeri looked up at the clock and frowned. "Should be here any moment, I think."

A moment later, the front door creaked open.

"Sounds like they heard you," I said.

Aeri rose and went to greet Declan, Connor, and Claire. The brother and sister pair had been in Puck's Glen with us just a few hours ago, and still looked beat-up and tired.

Claire's dark hair was still wet from her shower, and she wore a clean set of fighting leathers. As a mercenary for the Order of the Magica, she had an endless supply. She smiled, her eyes tired.

As usual, Connor wore an old band T-shirt. This one was emblazoned with the name *Lizzo*. A bag hung over his shoulder, no doubt full of potions ingredients.

I met his gaze. "Thank you for making this potion. Maybe Aeri and I could have handled it, but our specialty is the ones related to blood sorcery. This is too important to risk."

He grinned. "Any time."

"I just came as backup." Claire saluted.

"Well, we appreciate it." I gave Tarron a look. "He's pretty dangerous when he's conscious."

I went to the shelves, getting our last pair of manacles. It broke my heart to bind Tarron's wrists again, but until his mind was free of the false queen's influence, it had to be done.

Quickly, I bound his wrists in front of him. Aeri brought me a pillow to put under his head, and I smiled gratefully at her.

"Might as well leave him here." I turned to my friends. "Until he wakes up, at least."

"Hopefully I can get that antidote made before then," Connor said. "Declan explained the situation to me and showed me a picture of the recipe. Shouldn't take long."

"Thank you."

Connor strode to the main worktable that sat in the center of the room and put the bag on the table. As he unloaded it and got to work, I moved toward Claire. We stood side by side, watching Connor.

"How are you doing?" I asked.

"Good." She smiled at me, still looking weary. Her dark eyes were shadowed and her face pale.

Hell, I doubted I looked much better.

"You should be resting."

"Nah, I wanted to be here. I like Tarron. I want him to get better." She nudged me with her shoulder just slightly. "I like you, too. And this will be okay."

"Thanks." I smiled.

My gaze moved between Tarron and Connor, hoping that the potions master could move quickly. He combined several of his own ingredients with the root of Paeoria, grinding it all into a paste and then lighting it on fire. He collected the smoke in a glass bottle, then added a few more ingredients to turn it to liquid.

By the time he was done, my nerves were strung so tight that a loud noise could have shattered me.

He held up the bottle and smiled. "It's ready. He just has to drink it."

"Thanks." I strode toward him and took it, then knelt at Tarron's side.

Carefully, I lifted his head. He was still unconscious, and I shook him slightly.

He groaned and shifted, trapped in a dream state.

"He looks conscious enough to swallow," Aeri said. "Maybe get the potion in him before he fully wakes."

I grimaced, remembering the scene I'd walked in on earlier. Quickly, I moved Tarron's head farther upright, then tilted the vial of potion so a few drops seeped through his lips. He swallowed, never opening his eyes. I poured more in, holding my breath and praying he would swallow the rest. That it would work.

As I'd hoped, his throat moved. He swallowed the

potion, and I looked up at Connor. "How long until it works?"

"Should be instantaneous."

I shook Tarron slightly. "Come on, Tarron. Wake up now."

He jerked, his eyes flaring open.

Green.

His eyes were green.

Relief sagged my shoulders. *Thank fates.*

The yellow and black that indicated the false queen's possession were gone. Gratitude welled within me, making my eyes prick with tears.

Confusion flickered in his eyes, then he jerked away from me, moving back. His voice was harsh as he said, "Get away."

"What?" My heart twisted. "Tarron, we're trying to help you."

"I know that, damn it." His brow furrowed. "I'm dangerous. You need to stay away from me."

"You're *not*."

He raised his hands, the manacles clanking. "But I am, Mari."

The world closed in around us, until it felt like it was just the two of us in this room. "Not anymore. We've given you an antidote."

"I can still *feel* it, pulling at my soul. There's something within me that's *not* me. I couldn't live with myself if I hurt you."

"You won't."

He ignored the statement and stood, towering over me, his broad shoulders cutting out the light. "What happened?"

I stood. "You don't remember?"

"Bits and pieces."

"Let's sit for this."

I turned to face the others in the room, finding that chairs had appeared around the table. They must have gathered them while we were talking.

I sat. "We need to figure out what the hell is going on."

"And what the hell happened." He took a seat at the farthest end of the table, away from everyone else. I watched him with an aching heart.

Aeri and Claire sat next to me.

"Do you remember the battle when we tried to rescue Aeri and Declan from the false queen?" I asked. "How we fought her and her Unseelie minions in her tower?"

"Vaguely. She hit me with something, didn't she?"

"A curse," I said. "One that controls your soul."

He nodded, his eyes going dark and stormy. But not gold and black, thank fates. "I can feel her influence inside of me, fighting to break free. Whatever she did to me—it's slowly stealing my soul." He drew in a ragged breath. "It makes me do whatever she commands."

"Which is to kill me," I said.

He nodded, his gaze serious. "Whatever you've given me has helped, but I can still feel it. I don't have much time left."

"Until what?"

"Until my soul is gone for good. Then I am hers."

My stomach pitched.

"You can feel it that clearly?" Aeri asked.

He nodded. "Like it's leaking out and taking all of my spirit with it."

"And your magic," Declan said. "Is that correct?"

Tarron nodded. "Most likely. I haven't tried my power, but I have less of it, I think."

Damn it. This was all bad. Souls were everything in magic. Our power was linked to them.

"Soon, she'll have it all. My entire soul," Tarron said. "I can feel it."

It would be a fate worse than death. My heart twisted. "We're going to find a cure. I promise."

"What about the false queen?" he asked. "What if we kill her?"

"None of us are strong enough for that." I shook my head. "And even if we could manage it, it's a bad idea. Because your souls are linked, we think it could kill you, too."

"Damn it." He frowned. "And she wasn't injured in the battle?"

"Barely," Aeri said. "We slowed her a bit, but not for long."

I turned to Aeri. Because Tarron had been hit by the curse, we hadn't had a chance to talk about her imprisonment, but there could be clues there. "Did you learn anything while you were imprisoned?"

"She wanted you," Aeri said.

"To kill me or use me for my power?"

"Both." Aeri shrugged. "Whatever she could manage."

"And the people in her realm," Tarron said. "Do you have any idea how many are brainwashed to be on her side?"

"Not a clue." Aeri frowned. "It's hard to tell, to be honest. Her power is so strong."

"I know all too well." Tarron's tone was grim.

"We need to find a way to beat her," Aeri said.

"I'm not strong enough," I said. Aeri was immensely powerful, but this would be my job. I could feel it. And I just wasn't strong enough. "She's too fast with that power of hers."

"And once it hits you, you're done," Tarron said.

"We'll have help, though." I thought of the Unseelie we'd met in the forest when we'd been on the way to rescue Aeri. "There's a Resistance force in the forest. Unseelie who escaped her dark magic before they could be brainwashed."

Aeri leaned forward. "Really?"

I nodded. "They'll help us. They're eager to overthrow her."

"We'll help however we can," Claire said.

"Of course," Connor added.

"Thank you." I drew in a deep breath. "I need more magic. I already gave it everything I had to try to heal Tarron, and it didn't work. I could use my Dragon Blood to try to create my mother's light magic, but I know it won't work. I'm not strong enough."

"I don't think I can hit you with any more of that crazy white light," Claire said. "Whatever it was, I can't feel it inside myself. Not even a little."

I nodded, remembering the battle from a week ago. My mother and Claire had tangled, and unfamiliar magic had burst out of Claire. It had hit the false queen as a massive blast of light, and she'd grown stronger. "I know. I think that had as much to do with her as it did with you."

"Then what is your plan?" Connor asked.

You are only half of me. Half of what you could be. The false queen's last words to me echoed in my mind. They made my heart ache.

But what if I could use that?

Half of what you could be.

I needed to become more.

"What are you thinking?" Aeri asked.

My gaze flicked up to hers. "How could you tell I was thinking?"

"You've been staring into space for the last thirty seconds, and it's been dead silent all around." She gestured around the table.

Everyone was staring at me.

"Oh, right. Of course." Apparently, I was losing it.

But I was onto something. I knew it. "The false queen said that I was only half of her. Half of what I could be."

"Bitch," Aeri muttered.

Tarron growled low in his throat, and I shot them both a thankful look.

"But she's right. I'm not enough. Not as I am now. I need more magic."

Aeri frowned. "That's bullshit. You are enough."

I shook my head. "She said I am half of what she is. Half her power. So I need more. I need to become like her."

"Become like her?" Aeri asked. "That sounds terrible."

"Not evil. But stronger. As strong as her." Even as I said it, the slightest bit of doubt tugged at me. I didn't want to become like her.

But I did need to stop her.

I'd do anything to stop her.

Anything to heal Tarron.

If her magic had cursed him, I could heal him. I was her daughter, after all. So much of my magic was like hers —the mind control, the reflective power. I just needed to gain this magic as well.

"I'm not sure this is the right direction," Aeri said. "You're moving toward the darkness."

"Fight fire with fire, right?"

Aeri frowned, still unconvinced. "How are you going to do this?"

"I'm going to use my gift of premonition"—another gift that was like my mother's—"to find a way to become more powerful."

"I guess it's the only clue we have." Aeri sounded doubtful, but I waved her off. This would work.

It had to.

I couldn't call on specific information on command,

but I could often get clues related to a specific thing if I asked the right way.

The doorbell rang.

I frowned, then glanced at Aeri.

She shrugged. "No guests that I know of."

I stood and hurried to the door, then peaked out through the peephole.

Aethelred stood on the front step, wearing one of his familiar blue velour track suits. His long Gandalf beard blew in the wind, and brilliant blue eyes peered out of his wrinkled face. He stared right at me through the peephole. "I know you're in there, Mordaca. Open up."

I swung the door open and grinned. "It looks like your seer powers are still going strong."

"Of course." He stepped inside. "How do you think I knew you needed me?"

"Impressive. You could tell I was about to use my power?"

"Just got a feeling."

I grinned. "Thanks for coming."

His power would enhance mine. If we both looked into the future, our odds were better.

"I'll be expecting a walk on the beach for this."

I nodded. "Of course. As soon as I fix this little...issue, we'll get back to our Friday routine."

I'd missed my walks with Aethelred, so it would be no hardship.

I gestured for him to follow me into the workshop.

"Look what the cat dragged in," I said as we entered.

Wally, Aeri's hellcat, looked up from where he'd been sleeping on the mantel. His flame red eyes blazed, and the smoke wafting up from his fur moved more quickly. He meowed.

"He says he did no such thing," Aeri translated.

Only she could understand Wally, just like I was the only one who could interpret for Burn.

I grinned. "Sorry, Wally."

"Apologize to me, missy!" Aethelred said. "It takes quite a bit of effort to drag my old bones over here, so I'll be taking the credit, thank you very much."

I grinned at him. "Of course. My bad."

"Let's do this in front of the fire." He rubbed his back. "Getting a bit cold for me these days."

Tarron stood and dragged two chairs over to the fire.

Connor rose and walked to Aethelred. He carried his bag and rooted around inside for something. He stopped in front of us and pulled out a tiny vial that he handed to Aethelred. "Take this. It'll soothe your bones."

Aethelred squinted at it, looking suspicious. "You're not trying to poison me, are you, young man?"

Connor sputtered and Aethelred laughed.

The old man slapped him on the arm. "Just joshing, my boy."

Connor stopped sputtering, but he still looked awkward.

I nudged my old friend. "Say thank you, Aethelred."

"Thank you, boy." He uncorked the vial and swigged it back, then coughed. "Tastes like a dumpster."

Connor grinned. "That's how you know it's the real thing."

Aethelred stopped coughing and gave Connor a glare. "A little mint wouldn't hurt, you know."

I grimaced. "Mint garbage?"

"Better than plain garbage."

"We'll have to debate the merits of flavored garbage another time." I started toward the fire. "We've got a future to be seeing."

Aethelred joined me at the two chairs. We both sat, and the others gathered around. Tarron kept a few feet back from, seeming uncomfortable.

My heart ached for him. It was clear that he was worried that the queen's influence would overcome him.

"What are you looking for, my dear?" Aethelred asked. "I got the impression it has to do with your mother and this young man here." He nodded at Tarron. "But what specifically?"

"I need to figure out how to grow strong enough to heal Tarron and overthrow the false queen. She rules the Unseelie Court, but it is a reign of terror."

Aethelred nodded. "Two worthy goals."

Yeah, but finding the solution to both seemed impossible. Especially since I wanted them done ASAP.

He held out his gnarled hand, and I took it. Waves of his magic rolled over me, and I closed my eyes, calling upon my power. My magic rose within me, filling my soul.

I cast my mind into the future, asking my questions. Aethelred's power flowed into me, making my gift stronger.

As usual, the strange white clouds filled my mind's eye. Images rolled through, shadows amongst the clouds.

One called to me, and I approached. Through the mist, several figures appeared. Three of them stayed in the mist, but one approached so I could see her. She had crimson skin, bright as rubies, and wore a black gown that matched her ebony hair. Her face was indistinct, and massive amounts of power wafted off of her.

"Who are you?" I asked.

"Come to us." She raised her hand and sliced a blade across her palm.

White blood dripped to the ground.

I gasped.

Only one type of species had white blood.

Dragon Bloods.

I had to find the original Dragon Bloods.

4

But *how* did I find the original Dragon Bloods? And where?

The question made more clouds appear, more shadowy figures. The Dragon Bloods disappeared, and I was drawn toward another section of clouds. A massive building appeared in front of me, shadowed and mysterious.

The place was in ruins, but it was impossible to mistake. Tall pillars, amazing archways, long avenues of grass.

Rievaulx Abbey.

It was unmistakable. The enormous, ancient monastical structure was located in Northern England.

But why did I need to go there? I saw no Dragon Bloods amongst the ancient ruins. Just a few monks in plain cloaks.

Answers.

The white clouds faded, and I opened my eyes. Flames flickered in the hearth, and silence reigned.

Aethelred caught my gaze. "Well? What did you see?"

"The Dragon Bloods. It makes so much sense. I got most of my magic from them. And I need more. So of course we need to go to them."

Aeri still looked uncertain. "And you think they'll make you more like your mother?"

"They could make me stronger. Strong enough to drive away Tarron's curse and to defeat the false queen. Dragon Blood can make more magic. I didn't have enough—or mine isn't good enough, maybe—to gain the power to heal Tarron. But *they* could have that power."

"I'm not sure I like the sound of this," Aeri said.

"Do you have another plan?"

"No, damn it." She frowned. "Where are they?"

"I don't know. But I saw Rievaulx Abbey."

"The ruins?" Tarron asked. "The Dragon Bloods live there?"

"No, I think there will be answers there about how to find them."

"Yeah, I don't think it's meant to be easy," Aeri said. "They've always been basically...mythical."

"Yeah," Claire said. "If I hadn't met you guys, I'd still be skeptical."

"If this is our plan, we need to go right away," Aeri said.

"You should lock me up while you're gone," Tarron said. "Leave a guard."

I glared. "Hell no. You have to come with us."

He frowned. "It's too dangerous for you to be around me."

My heart ached at the pain in his voice. "It'll be fine. You need to be there in case they can give me enough power to cure you."

"How do you know you'll find the cure there?" he asked.

"I *feel* it. The way that I feel anything that is true in my visions." It was mostly true. I could sense that something important would happen there—I just prayed that it would be fixing Tarron.

His jaw tightened. "I'll go. I admit that I want to keep my soul. But it needs to be more than just you and me." His gaze moved to Aeri. "Come with us. Please. I can feel the false queen's grip on my soul. If this temporary anti-dote stops working and I succumb, I don't want Mari to be alone with me." His gaze moved to Declan. "You, too."

I knew what Tarron was thinking. He was immensely powerful. If he lost control of himself, he wanted someone there who wouldn't hesitate to take him out. I would definitely hesitate. Aeri probably would, too, because she knew I loved him.

Declan wouldn't hesitate.

He liked me, but he'd be more inclined to keep me alive and worry about the state of my heart later.

"I insist." Tarron's tone was firm. "Please."

"We'll do it," Aeri said.

"Thank you." I looked at Declan. "We need someone to keep an eye on the false queen. To make connections with the Resistance, if possible. Because once we're done with the Dragon Bloods, I'm coming for her."

"I can send Luna," Tarron said.

Claire leaned forward. "Connor and I can help."

"Are you sure?" I asked. "You've already done so much. You must be exhausted."

"Of course I'm sure. I want to help. Anyway, I'm curious about her, too." She shrugged. "And if I need backup, I'm sure the FireSouls would step in."

"Thank you." I reached out and squeezed her hand.

"I think you need to rest, though," Claire said. "You all look like hell."

I couldn't remember the last time I'd slept, so I was sure she was right. Tarron and I had gone straight from escaping hell to rescuing Aeri and him getting cursed.

"Just a few hours," Aeri said. "Then we'll take off."

I looked at Tarron, who nodded. Even he had shadows under his eyes.

"Fine." I stood. "Claire, Connor, thank you."

"Anytime," Connor said.

I gave Claire a small vial of my blood that she could use to open the portal to the Unseelie Realm. As she took it and tucked it into her pocket, I wished I were going with her. I hated the idea that my friends were walking into that dangerous realm alone just to help me.

Claire squeezed my hand. "It'll be fine. Worth it."

"Thanks."

They departed, and Aeri and Declan headed to her apartment.

Tarron and I stood, staring at each other. My gaze dropped to the manacles at his wrist.

I stepped forward, reaching for them. "Damn. I forgot those. I'm sorry."

He stepped back. "I'll keep them on while we rest."

"No. That's terrible."

His lips thinned and his brow creased. Pain flashed in his eyes. "You don't get it, Mari. I can *feel* her in my soul."

I strode toward him and placed my hands on his jaw. "You're strong enough to fight her."

"Maybe. But I won't risk you."

I scowled at him, but my heart softened. "I can't believe this happened."

He bowed his head, leaning over to rest his forehead on mine. "I'd rather it be me than you."

"Don't you get it? I'd prefer the same thing. I hate to see you like this. Suffering."

"We'll have to agree to disagree."

"Fine." I tilted my head up and pressed my mouth to his.

He groaned low in his throat and captured my lips. I leaned into the kiss, every inch of me heating as he kissed me like his life depended on it. He grabbed my hands with his, pulling me until I was pressed against his front. His bound hands got in the way, but I didn't care. I pressed myself close and enjoyed every second.

With a pained groan, he pulled away. "I don't want to lose control. She could slip in while I'm distracted by you."

Damn it. I didn't want to let him go.

Still, I respected his wishes, backing up just slightly.

"What are we going to do?" I asked.

"What do you mean?"

"When we get you fixed and we stop her, we suddenly have two kingdoms on our hands. Neither of us asked for them."

His gaze turned serious. "We didn't."

"You've done a great job ever since the death of your brother. But..."

"You don't want it."

"No."

"I don't blame you." He dragged a hand over his face. "You would have to give up your entire life here—no question. I've been neglecting my kingdom while we've been on this hunt. And it is worth it. But the work is piling up."

I drew in a shuddery breath, trying not to think of all the issues I would face. I didn't want to leave Aeri. I didn't want to live in a different realm from Tarron. My time would be split between the Unseelie Court, the Seelie Court, and Magic's Bend.

That was no life.

And I had no idea how to fix it.

"We need to rest." His gaze flicked to mine, and the green appeared darker with pain. "I fear exhaustion. If I weaken, her hold could grow stronger. And you need to stop worrying about this."

Frustration surged within me, but I had to agree. I wouldn't do anything to risk him. "Let's go rest. But in the same bed."

"Not a chance." His tone was firm. "There needs to be a locked door between me and you. Especially since you'll be vulnerable in sleep."

I scowled. But he wasn't going to budge. "Fine. Let's go."

The dream hit me—hard and fast.

Tarron, going for my throat. His eyes flashed with hate as he surged toward me, covering the ground quickly. I darted backward, trying to avoid him.

But the hate in his eyes wasn't him. No, it was the false queen. As he closed in on me, she stood behind him, a victorious glare on her face.

"I will find you, daughter." Her voice echoed with frost. "I'd hoped you would join me, but I was wrong."

"Never," I hissed, darting out of the way of Tarron's attack.

He was slow—slow in the way of dreams, when things happen as if you are seeing them through a lens made of water.

"He is mine now, and he will stop at nothing to kill you," she hissed.

"I will cure him." I darted left, avoiding his grasp. "And I will beat you."

"You'll never be as strong as me."

"I will. And I will take the Unseelie Court from you. Your reign of terror ends."

She cackled. "You are half of me, and you have no idea the plans I have put into place."

I jerked out of the dream, woken by my alarm. Cold sweat dotted my forehead, and I sat up, panting. My heart raced as I searched my bedroom, looking for Tarron. Looking for his attack.

"No," I muttered. "Just a dream. Just a dream."

But part of it had been real. That had been the false queen—no doubt. She'd used dreams to send me messages before, and she was doing it again.

But she was wrong. I'd become strong enough. I'd become as strong as her.

Aeri's words echoed in my mind... *You're moving toward darkness.*

But I wasn't. I just needed to gain power like hers so I could fight fire with fire. Right now, I wasn't enough.

But I could be. I would beat her and save my people. Save Tarron's people.

Still shaking, I climbed out of bed and dressed.

I'd only gotten a few hours' sleep—and they'd sucked —but I was feeling better. Faster, more alert. I changed quickly into fight wear, then yanked my hair up into a quick bouffant ponytail and streaked the black makeup around my eyes.

Grimly, I stared into the mirror.

I'd moved so fast and aggressively with my black makeup that it looked more like a mask than ever. Streaks of black paint winged out from my eyes.

Good.

I looked like a crazed warrior of old, and that's what I was going for.

I entered the living room to find Tarron sitting up from the couch. His arms were still bound in front of him.

Shadows lingered in his eyes, and his wrists were covered in blood.

"What's wrong with your wrists?" I asked, even as the horrible idea began to form.

"She's strong, Mari." His voice was rough.

"Her influence came to you in the night." I thought of the dream.

"I fought it off, but..." He stood and raised his hands, showing his bloody wrists.

She'd made him try to break free.

To get to me.

"You can take those off now, though," I said.

He frowned. "I don't know if that's a good idea."

"We're both awake. Aware. We can fight her if she comes to you. Anyway, I need you fighting by my side."

His jaw tightened and his eyes looked tortured.

"I can look out for myself," I said. "And Aeri and Declan will be with us, like you requested."

"Fine." He nodded his head sharply. "But you must swear to strike to kill if her influence overtakes me."

I bit my tongue, not wanting to make that promise.

"Mari...I know you're strong enough to take care of yourself. But you have to be willing to."

"Willing to hurt you, you mean?"

"Not me. *Her.* When she is in my mind, I am nothing but a shell. And I *will* kill you if she takes control."

"The potion helps, though."

"It does, which is the only reason I'm willing to take these cuffs off. Now *promise me*."

"I'll aim to kill." It was probably a lie, but he seemed to buy it.

"Good."

I walked to him and quickly sliced my fingertip with my sharp thumbnail, then swiped the blood across the metal. The cuffs unlocked.

"That's dangerous," he said. "If I get your blood, I can unlock myself?"

"I have to give it willingly."

"Clever."

"Always." I swallowed hard. "My mother came to me in a dream. She's putting some big plans into place."

"Any idea what they are?"

"No, but we should tell Claire and Luna what they're walking into in the Unseelie Court."

He nodded. "I'll call Luna and tell her. While they're making contact with the Resistance, they can try to figure out what she is doing."

"Thanks. Let me get us some food, and we'll meet Aeri and Declan."

He followed me into the kitchen, and I thought how nice it would be to just live here normally with him. Or live anywhere normally with him. I couldn't imagine leaving Darklane and Aeri, even though she was only here half the time because of Declan.

But Tarron was the king of an entire separate realm. And I was the queen of another.

Oof. Those were some responsibilities I didn't want to face now.

"Is a bacon sandwich all right with you?" I asked.

"Who would turn down bacon?"

"A vegetarian."

Tarron laughed.

"Also a vegan." I shot a look at him, glad to see at least part of a smile on his face. "It'll have to be microwaved. We don't have time for more."

"It'll do. Thanks." He leaned against the counter and looked at me. "Are you all right?"

"Fine. Don't worry about me." I shifted under the weight of his gaze, then turned to the fridge and began rustling inside of it. I'd been eating these a lot lately, but it was major comfort food.

He grumbled in a low tone, "I always worry about you."

I looked back over my shoulder at him. "Well, you don't have to."

"It comes with the territory."

"Territory?"

"Of loving you."

"Oh." I warmed, my heart thundering.

Then my eyes began to prick with tears. Worried tears, not happy tears. There was so much at stake here. And I had no idea how—*if*—we could fix this.

Why did it have to get all sweet and loving right before it was meant to go to shit?

Burn appeared at my side, pressing his thorny body

against my legs. It was as if he'd sensed I'd needed a bit of support.

I sucked in a deep breath and leaned against him, then set myself to the task of making sandwiches. Ignoring Tarron's last words was the only way I was going to keep it together, so I went with that option.

Ten minutes later, we had three sandwiches—one for me, one for Tarron, and one for my emotional support wolf.

We met Aeri and Declan in the main part of the foyer. As usual, Aeri was dressed in her white fight wear—her ghost suit, as she called it, since it allowed her to become invisible. Her sleek blond hair was pulled back in a ponytail, and she looked ready for battle.

Declan wore dark, sturdy clothes that were perfect for fighting. His longish dark hair was still a bit messy from sleep, but his eyes were alert.

"Ready to do this?" Aeri asked.

"Beyond ready." I looked between the three of them. "I can transport us in two rounds."

They nodded. I took Aeri and Declan first, gripping each of their hands and calling upon my magic. The ether sucked us in and spun us through space, spitting us out in the cold misty morning in northern England. We stood in a forest near the medieval town of York. It was still dark, but birds were beginning to chirp. Massive trees surrounded us, and the quiet of the forest was welcoming and creepy at the same time.

We were far enough north that it was quite cold. It

wasn't yet dawn, but it was close. I could sense the arrival of the sun, a new Fae talent I wasn't used to yet.

I caught Aeri's eye. "I'll be back in a sec."

She nodded, and I returned to Magic's Bend and picked up Tarron. By the time the ether spat us back out in England, my nerves were humming with anticipation.

Mist rolled along the ground, snaking between the trees.

Aeri rubbed her arms. "We're in a valley of some kind. Where is the old abbey?"

I called upon my Seeker sense, asking it to help me find the abbey. I hadn't wanted to put us right on the doorstep in case our sudden arrival alerted someone to our presence. The abbey should be an abandoned ruin, but that didn't mean there weren't ghosts.

My Seeker sense tugged toward the left, and I pointed. "I think it's that way. Not far."

The four of us started through the woods, tromping between the trees. I rubbed my arms, colder than I'd expected.

Tarron's magic flared briefly, and he handed me a leather jacket that he'd conjured.

"Thanks." I took it and slipped it on, immediately warmer. "Nice choice. You have good taste."

"I thought it would suit you."

I could get used to a life of him giving me things he thought would suit me. I smiled at him and kept going.

We reached the edge of the forest, and I stopped, staring in awe at the enormous building in front of us.

Hills rose on either side of the fantastical structure. The enormous old abbey was illuminated in the pale gray light of dawn.

It was an incredible structure of pillars and arches, statues and stained glass. Now, it stood as a ruin, with parts of the ceiling and walls missing. That only served to highlight the graceful lines and beautiful architecture, however.

"I can't believe they let it fall into ruin," I murmured.

"Henry VIII," Declan said. "He destroyed many holy structures while he was trying to enforce his own religion."

I shook my head, not surprised. "Let's go."

As we crept toward the ruins, I kept my senses alert for ghosts. The mist drifted over the ground, silent and creepy, but I saw no ghosts. A little village surrounded the abbey, but it was quiet as the grave. We skirted around it, heading right for the ruined building.

"No one lives here," Tarron said. "These houses feel empty."

"Agreed," Aeri said.

I perked my ears, but heard nothing from within the structures. They didn't look like they were in a state of abandoned disrepair, but I had to agree with Tarron and Aeri. Something had driven these people away.

I shivered and kept going, my eyes on the huge structure ahead of us. It was more than one building—or at least, it had been. Once upon a time, it would have been an enormous complex bustling with monks. Now it was a maze of broken walls and different levels of grass flooring that had replaced the tiled ground.

We stepped between the first set of walls, and the heavy weight of history bore down upon me. So much had happened here, so long ago.

"What are we looking for?" Aeri asked.

"I have no idea," I said. "My vision wasn't very clear."

"Do you feel that?" Tarron tilted his head. "We're not alone."

I shivered. "Yeah. It's like we're being watched."

Tarron called upon his wings, and crackling lightning flared behind his back, brilliant and beautiful. He launched himself into the air and surveyed from above. I closed my eyes and sniffed, but got no hint of magic from other supernaturals. I couldn't hear anything out of the ordinary either. Just early morning birdsong.

Declan called upon his fallen angel wings, the black feathers were tipped in silver. He shot toward the sky, joining Tarron in his aerial survey.

Aeri tilted her head back and stared up at them. "They look pretty good, huh?"

I followed her gaze, catching sight of the two men. The morning had turned pale gray as the sun approached the horizon, so there was enough light to see them well. They were graceful and powerful all at once, both too handsome to be real.

"Yeah." I shook my head, trying to get my focus back. "I don't think anyone is here."

"Neither do I," Aeri said. "Just an abandoned village and ruined church."

"Then why do I feel them?"

Tarron and Declan joined us a moment later, landing gracefully on brilliant green grass in front of us.

"I saw nothing," Tarron said.

"Same. We're alone here."

I frowned. We needed to learn something from this place, and it clearly wasn't going to come from people. "Let's look for a clue. Something inscribed on a wall maybe, or buried under the ground."

"We should spread out," Aeri said.

"But stay within sight of each other," Tarron added.

As everyone scattered, I called upon my Seeker sense, asking it to find me a clue. How was this place linked to the Dragon Bloods? How could we find them?

My magic tugged, so slightly that I almost couldn't feel it. Almost like it was instinct more than anything. I followed the pull down the grassy lane, walking between the tall pillars of stone that had once formed a fantastic corridor.

All three of my companions were within eyesight as they stuck close to the building walls, looking for a clue. I followed them, diverging into a smaller stone room that had most of the walls still standing but no roof.

It led to a huge chamber that had probably once been the main worship hall. An enormous stone altar stood at one end, majestic in the early morning light. Flowers grew around it, their buds opening beneath the dew.

I hurried toward the altar, spotting a carving in the stone at the base.

What the heck was it?

As I knelt by it, Tarron joined me.

"That's the first possible clue I've seen so far." He crouched at my side. "But what does it mean?"

I squinted at the squiggles. The inscription was so old and worn that it was impossible to say if it was writing or an image.

Aeri knelt at my side, staring hard at the faded artwork. "In pagan times, altars were for sacrifices."

"This is a Christian church, though," I said.

Declan appeared behind the altar, studying the surface with a frown.

I caught his eye. "You're a fallen angel. This has got to be your area. What do you think?"

"Aeri isn't wrong. And there were periods when local Christian sects adopted some pagan traditions as a way of influencing those people to join."

"So you're saying we should make a sacrifice?"

He shrugged. "Can't hurt."

I frowned. "I'm not about to sacrifice an animal on here. I can tell you that much."

"There's not much more than squirrels around here anyway," he said.

"I'm *definitely* not doing that to some poor hapless squirrel." I searched my mind. "But I like this idea. Being a Dragon Blood is all about your blood, right?"

"So, we should spill a bit here," Aeri said.

"It's worth trying," Tarron added.

I sliced my fingertip with my sharp thumbnail and swiped a bit of blood across the top of the altar.

Nothing happened.

"Damn." I swiped some blood across the faded stone carving.

Still nothing.

"Let me try," Aeri said.

I nodded, watching her cut her finger and drip a few brilliant white dots onto the stone surface. We were both Dragon Bloods, but only she had the pure white blood that was commonly associated with the species. My black blood had been modified—I didn't like the word *tainted*, even though it came to mind—by my Unseelie heritage.

When nothing happened, Aeri swiped her bleeding finger across the stone inscription.

Magic sparked on the air.

I stumbled back, watching as the stone *grew*. The faded inscription became clearer, almost like time was turning backward. The wear and tear of the ages was being reversed.

"I still can't read it," Aeri said.

"It's gibberish," Tarron added.

They were right. Whatever language the words were in, I couldn't read it. They were much clearer now, though.

"Guys..." Declan's voice was tinged with warning. "We're not alone anymore."

5

I WHIRLED AROUND, SPOTTING THE BACK OF A FIGURE cloaked in a simple brown robe.

Whatever that inscription said, clearly it had done its job. The ancient monk had appeared out of nowhere, and now stood facing away from us, so he hadn't seen us yet.

"Crap!" I hissed.

Tarron lunged behind the altar, joining Declan. I followed, along with Aeri.

The four of us crouched behind the huge stone altar and peered over the top.

I caught sight of the roof overhead and whispered, "That wasn't there before."

Aeri jerked her head to the left. "Neither was that wall."

"Or that monk," Tarron added. "And he's partially transparent."

"We've brought this place back from the past," Declan said.

I whistled low under my breath. "Cool spell."

"No wonder we didn't feel like we were alone." Aeri peeked up from behind the altar to get a closer look.

A few more monks filed into the room, immediately turning away from us to do something along the far wall. I couldn't figure out what it was, but it was giving us a short time to get the hell away from here.

"Let's go." I sprinted to the door nearest us, darting inside.

My friends followed, joining me in the little hallway that hadn't existed just a few minutes ago. It was dark and empty, thank fates. Instead of the usual grass ground, the tile floor had returned from the past. It had been painted with ornate designs, reminding me of the wealth of the ancient churches.

"So maybe a person actually *is* going to tell us about the Dragon Bloods," I said. "Now that they're here, that is."

"Which one, though?" Aeri asked.

"We should speak to the abbot," Declan said. "They generally know the most in a place like this."

"And the location of the Dragon Bloods would be some high-ranking info," Aeri said.

"But why would an abbot of a medieval Christian church know about the Dragon Bloods?" I asked. "They aren't a religious group."

"They were medieval holders of knowledge and locations of power," Declan said. "No doubt the Dragon Bloods are an ancient group. It makes sense that religious organizations would know of them. In fact, I doubt the Christians are the only ones who know where they are."

"But they're the closest ones to us right now," I said. "So let's go find that abbot."

"Any idea where he'd be hanging out in a place like this?" Aeri asked.

"Nicer quarters, of course," Declan said. "Not the barracks the regular monks call home. It would be private. A tower of some sort, most likely."

"I can try my Seeker sense. Look for the abbot and a tower."

Everyone nodded.

I called upon my power, envisioning an old abbot in a tower. It took a moment, but it tugged on me eventually. I gasped, then pointed down the hall. "That way."

We started down the hall, past windows empty of glass that provided a view over the fields below. Monks in rough woolen robes tended to the vegetable patches, toiling under the early morning sun.

"Laborer monks," Declan said. "Uneducated, but they serve the lord with their work."

We moved quickly and silently through the halls, keeping our ears alert to our surroundings. The monks were early risers, and it seemed most were at work. At one point, we passed an enormous room filled with small desks. Monks sat hunched over them, transcribing books. The entire place was deathly silent.

We passed through wide hallways and twisting corridors, trying to avoid any ghosts we might come across.

We got unlucky near the kitchens.

A monk carrying a big tureen exited a door and nearly collided with us. His eyes widened, and he shouted in an unintelligible language. English...almost.

But the message was clear.

"Run," I said.

The four of us sprinted past the monk. My Seeker sense dragged us down the hall, pulling me toward the abbot in his tower. There was a loud clattering sound behind us, and I knew it had to be the tureen smashing to the ground.

I glanced behind, just in time to see the monk thrust out a hand and shoot a blast of light at us.

"Duck!" I dived low, narrowly avoiding the shot of magic.

My friends followed suit.

The magic slammed into the wall in front of us, chipping the stone.

"Damn, they're serious about protecting this place," Aeri muttered.

No wonder they knew the location of the Dragon Bloods. They were *magical* monks.

I scrambled upright and looked back. Three more ghosts had joined our attacker. They sprinted for us.

"Move!" I raced ahead, determined not to launch an attack. They were just protecting their turf. No way I was going to hurt a bunch of old men of god.

My friends seemed to agree. We sprinted down the

hall, dodging and darting. As we turned the corner in the hall, Burn appeared at my side.

"Go scare them!" I commanded. "But *don't* hurt them!"

Burn gave a low woof of understanding, and careened around, sprinting toward the monks. I looked back to see him crouch and growl. The monk's blasts of magic hit him, and he only grew stronger, vibrating with energy and joy.

Burn loved shit like this.

The four monks skidded to a halt, their brown robes flapping around their legs as their eyes widened in shock.

They shouted, words I didn't understand but their meaning was clear enough.

Burn was a hell dog to them, and they didn't like him.

"Look where you're going!" Aeri shouted.

I turned back just in time to see some stairs rising up ahead of us.

"Crap!" I leapt onto them, avoiding tripping.

"Is the abbot up there?" Tarron asked.

"I think so." My magic tugged strongly, directing me that way.

Three different monks appeared from a hall to our right. A flash of brown alerted me to their presence, and I turned in time to see them shout and raise their hands.

"Go!" I sprinted up the stairs, calling upon my wings as I went. The staircase was wide enough that I could fly, and damned if I wouldn't take advantage of the power. Outrunning monks and their magic was freaking hard.

Tarron joined me, while Aeri and Declan stayed on their feet. They were both massively fast, outrunning the monks by just enough that the stairs exploded behind them.

I flapped my wings, flying as fast as I could to the huge wooden door at the top. It was closed, shut tight against us.

Tarron put on a burst of speed and flew into it, blasting it open. The four of us tumbled inside the room, and Declan whirled around, slamming the door shut and leaning against it.

An old man in ornate crimson and gold robes surged to his feet by the fire, his watery eyes going wide. "What are you doing?"

I could barely make out his words. It was definitely some old form of English.

"We need help." I landed and folded my wings back into my body. The monks here had magic, so the abbot didn't look shocked by my Fae traits.

He scowled. "Then ask, do not destroy."

Tarron glanced back at the door, where the latch was broken. Declan stood with his back against it, keeping it shut.

"I apologize," Tarron said.

The abbot harrumphed. He looked small in the dark room. There were no windows, which was weird as hell, and it was lit only by the fire. The rug was of nice quality, and the tapestries on the wall gave it a warm feeling. But it was otherwise completely empty. For prayer, perhaps?

"We are looking for the location of the Dragon Bloods," I said. "I saw in a vision of the future that I would find that information here."

His brows lowered. "I don't have that information."

"Yes, you do," Tarron said. "You're a terrible liar."

The abbot flushed red. "I am not a liar. A man of god would never lie."

I didn't bother telling him that was a load of bullshit.

His gaze flicked toward me, and it looked almost like recognition flickered within his eyes.

I frowned at him.

Aeri strode toward him, drawing a dagger from the ether. The abbot shrank back.

"I'm not going to hurt you." She sliced her own palm and held it out to him, showing him the white blood. "Look. I am one of them. We do not seek to hurt them."

His gaze flicked to us, lingering on me a bit longer. "What about them? Are they Dragon Bloods as well?"

Shit. I couldn't prove it with my black blood. And Tarron and Declan definitely weren't.

"We mean them no harm," I said. "Our realms are in desperate danger if I cannot find the Dragon Bloods."

"I know nothing of what you speak." The determination in his voice worried me.

This guy was not going to give the info up easily. But he kept looking at me funny.

"Do you know me?"

"What?" He flapped his hands, a strange gesture. "Of course not!"

Hmmmm.

Pounding sounded on the door.

"That will be my monks," the abbot said. "Leave here and we will not harm you."

"We can't go without the information we seek," Tarron said.

"Well, I am not giving it!"

He meant it.

I strode toward him, slicing my fingertip with my sharp thumbnail. As pain spiked and blood welled, I hoped this power could work on a ghost.

He flinched back from me.

I moved quickly, swiping my bloody fingertip against his forehead. Magic flared, and I looked into his eyes, giving my voice a hit of power that I hoped would influence him. "You will answer our questions."

His eyes went hooded and his shoulders relaxed. "I will answer your question."

Victory surged through me. "Thank you. Now, where do we find the Dragon Bloods?"

"On the Slate Isles." He spoke with the slowness of the magically influenced.

"Where are those?" I asked.

"West coast of Scotland.

Tarron frowned. "There are hundreds of islands out there. Which ones?"

"I do not know."

"Crap." I looked at my friends. "He means it."

"None of us know," the abbot said. "This place is ancient. Abandoned so long that none of us know the current location of the Dragon Bloods."

"So they move?" I asked.

"To avoid detection, yes. We were the original holders of that information, but no longer."

"But someone knows." I leaned a bit closer to him. "Who? Is that the information you protect? The secret-bearer's location?"

Something strange flickered in his eyes. They focused on me, so intense I wanted to step backward. I resisted. "You will find that information in the nearest city. York. A place with enough magic that it can support the ghost of a Dragon Blood."

"A *real* Dragon Blood?" I asked. "One of the originals?"

"Not an original, no. They are immortal. But you will find the answers you seek in this man."

"Where is he in the city?"

"Within the city walls."

That didn't answer much, as the entire city of York was contained within the medieval walls.

The pounding on the doors grew stronger. More frantic.

"There are more of them," Declan grunted. "Can't hold it much longer."

Shit.

We needed to get out of here.

Hopefully, I called upon my transportation magic, but found myself blocked by a protection charm.

"My transport power doesn't work. We have to run." I whirled around, but there was no escape within. Not a single window.

I glanced back at the abbot, whose eyes had cleared. Crap, he was no longer under my spell.

"Time's up," I said. "We have as much as we're going to get."

Tarron moved to stand about ten feet in front of Declan, who still held the door in place.

"Move to the side on my count," Tarron said.

Declan nodded.

"Three, two, one." Tarron nodded.

Declan lunged to the left. The door flew open, and a half dozen monks piled in, with more following. Tarron raised his hand, and a gust of air billowed forth from his palms. It bowled into the monks, who tumbled over, creating a path for us.

"Go!" Tarron shouted.

Aeri, Declan, and I raced through the empty space and down the stairs, jumping over fallen monks as we fled.

"Defend your home!" The old abbot's words rang out after us.

Was he really asking these old monks to fight?

Ahead of us, stones shot out from the wall. The rocks hurtled toward us, and I ducked low, avoiding a blow to the head.

"Holy crap, he's gotten the abbey to fight us!" Aeri said.

The building *itself* was mounting an offense.

Beneath my feet, the stone stairs began to shake, then fall away. I nearly tripped and went down, saving myself at the last minute with a powerful jump. I called upon my wings, feeling them flare to life behind me. As the stairs disappeared, I launched myself into the air. Tarron joined me. Declan called upon his own wings, sweeping Aeri up into his arms. She could fly, but it was an incredibly difficult magic, and when she transformed, she was freaking enormous. So big she'd have destroyed the abbey itself.

The four of us flew down the stairs and through the massive hall. The huge main room where we'd entered was now full of beautiful stained glass. It exploded inward at us, sending shards of colorful glass hurtling through the air.

The projectiles sliced across my skin, leaving burning wounds. I called upon two shields, holding them at each side to avoid the cuts. Still, the glass hit my wings, and I was faltering as I neared the exit.

"Keep going!" Tarron shouted.

I pushed myself harder, desperate to reach the outside. As soon as we got away from the abbey, my magic could transport us. I just had to make it fifty more yards.

The whole building began to shake around us.

"Watch out!" Aeri shouted.

A massive pillar fell toward Tarron. He dived, his powerful wings carrying him out of the way. The pillar slammed into the ground, shattering the mosaic tile floor. Sections of the roof began to fall, a huge one nearly crushing me. It clipped my wing, sending me into a spin.

"Mari!" Tarron grabbed my arm, stopping my free fall, and my wings caught the air once more.

"This place will crush us!" I flew as fast as I could. Almost there. Almost.

My heart thundered and my muscles ached. Dust and debris filled the air as the building collapsed around us. Another pillar crashed to the ground, falling right through the two huge wooden doors, leaving an open space for us.

We hurtled through, flying out of the massive abbey just as the entire thing crashed to the ground behind us.

I skidded to a stop on the grass, pain and exhaustion making me roll haphazardly. I scrambled upright, turning around to see the ghostly piles of rubble. Some of the walls still stood, soaring toward the sky, a beautiful ruin.

Shocked, I stood. "They destroyed the place to get to us."

Tarron joined me, limping slightly due to a huge cut on his thigh.

Declan set Aeri on the ground. Both looked like hell.

"It's not destroyed," Declan said.

I blinked.

He was right. The part of the building that was still standing was the part that had been standing when we'd first arrived. As I watched, the ghostly rubble began to disappear, leaving only the verdant green grass that glowed emerald under the light of the early morning sun.

"The ruins have put themselves back to rights," Tarron said.

There were no monks charging out to attack us. No more ghosts.

And we'd gotten what we'd come for.

I eyed the horrible wound on Tarron's leg, and

approached. Without saying anything, I touched his shoulder and fed my new healing energy into him.

"You've always healed me before," I said. "Time to return the favor."

"Thank you." He frowned. "You're hurt, too."

I shrugged. My own wounds hurt like hell.

He pressed his hands gently to my shoulders and fed his healing energy into me. It surged through my veins, warm and comforting.

My gaze collided with his, and it was like the rest of the world disappeared around us. Birdsong faded and the world narrowed until I could only see him. His beautiful green eyes.

They'd once been gold and black—and they might be again—but for now, he was here. With me. I'd take what I could get, and enjoy it.

As his warmth flowed through me, the pain faded. My skin knit itself back together, and finally, I was whole.

The wound on his leg finally closed, and I withdrew my hand. I turned around and spotted Declan healing Aeri. Her white fight suit was covered in red blood from her wounds. It was a gruesome sight, the product of a spell that turned her white blood red when it touched the fabric of the suit. We didn't tell anyone what we were, and the spell definitely helped.

When they were done, they turned to me.

"I can transport us." I nodded to Declan and Aeri. "You two first."

They approached, reaching for my hand. We gripped

each other, and I closed my eyes, envisioning a distinct place within the city walls of York—Clifford's Tower.

The motte and bailey castle was impossible to miss—a simple tower extending up from a hill—one where terrible things had once happened.

It seemed perfect for the present state of affairs.

The three of us appeared within the tower. It was a nearly-round space, only about a hundred feet in diameter, with soaring white stone walls and an open ceiling. It had once been the scene of a terrible genocide, when the Christians had attacked the Jews in York, besieging them in the tower until they'd collectively committed suicide to avoid a terrible fate outside of the castle walls.

Aeri glanced at it. "Interesting choice."

"I thought it would be empty at this hour." And I was right. There wasn't a soul around. No one to see us appear out of thin air. "I'll be right back."

I returned to the abbey and found Tarron staring at the ruins, shadows in his eyes. He turned to me as I approached. "I can feel her influence more strongly."

I shivered, cold rolling over me.

I could feel it too. Like I was looking into the false queen's eyes.

"Fight it."

"I am. I will." His jaw tightened. "But I can feel that there may come a time when I am not strong enough, despite my best efforts."

"There won't."

"There *will*. And if you are there and I attack, you must strike to kill. You *must*."

A shiver raced over me as I remembered the terrible dream I'd had. He was right. When he was like that, he couldn't be reasoned with.

"We'll face that problem when it comes." I gripped his hand. "For now, you're here. And we're going to fix this."

His lips tightened, but he just nodded. There was no point in arguing with me about this. No point at all.

6

I transported Tarron and myself to Clifford's Tower. The city was just waking up, but here, inside the tower, it was quiet.

A dark energy filled the air, and I shuddered. "Let's get the hell out of here."

"It's haunted," Aeri said. "No question."

I shivered. After our last encounter with ghosts, I wasn't keen to see more. Especially not here at the tower, where such horrible things had happened so long ago.

We hurried to the iron gates. Quickly, Aeri picked the lock, and we slipped out of the tower. Clifford's Tower was a motte and bailey castle, which meant it was essentially just a simple tower built on top of a man-made mound of earth.

In front of us, a long row of stairs extended down the hill to the ground. We hurried down, bypassing some geese who seemed determined to cause trouble. We were on the outskirts of the oldest part of town, and it felt dead.

"I don't think that what we seek is here," Tarron said.

I nodded. "Let's head farther into the city."

We walked toward the ancient buildings of York. It didn't take long to reach the twisting, cobblestone walkways of the main part of the city. The buildings were ancient, medieval things that leaned drunkenly into each other. They were pressed so close to one another that the streets were narrow and winding. Ancient cobblestones lined the ground.

Once I stood amongst the historical jumble, there was more for my Seeker sense to pick up on.

Except it didn't really work.

There was *too* much here.

"Any luck?" Aeri asked.

"No. I can feel a general tug in that direction"—I pointed down the street—"but there's so many buildings crammed together that I can't tell which one the ghost is in."

"Lot of ghosts here," Declan said.

"What about this place?" Tarron pointed to a hanging sign above us. "We might be able to narrow it down in there."

I looked up, catching sight of the cursive words *Medieval Museum of York*. "A museum?"

"They should have old maps that could give us clues about which buildings to check," he said.

"Oh, not a bad plan."

"And a nice change from running from ghosts," Aeri said.

We entered the quiet little museum and paid the fare, then entered the silent exhibits.

"Let's split up," Aeri whispered. "I'll call you if we find anything promising."

"Sounds good." I gave a little wave as she and Declan melted into the darkness, disappearing into the dioramas exhibit.

Tarron and I went the other way, walking down aisles of glass cabinets filled with artifacts, each painstakingly marked with little paper cards. They didn't seem promising, so I headed toward another exhibit. We needed maps.

The museum was empty at that hour, with not a single soul around. It was almost soothing.

I leaned toward him. "This is surprisingly *normal* for us."

"Almost like a date," Tarron said.

"You'd take me to a museum on a date?"

"Literally anywhere on a date would be good with you."

I smiled up at him.

He grinned down at me, but his smile faltered. He grimaced and staggered, gasping, "Get away."

Oh no.

His eyes went gold, shot through with black.

"Tarron." I gripped his arms. "Come back to me."

He groaned, his fists clenching. "Get back."

"No. Fight it!"

His face twisted, and he shuddered.

"You can do this." I shoved him back against a wall, hard enough that his head smacked.

He just growled lower.

I pressed myself against him, kissing him as hard as I could.

He went still, then pulled back, gasping.

His eyes were green once more.

"Are you all right?" he asked. "Did I hurt you?"

"No."

"That was too close."

"We're also getting closer to a solution. A permanent one. I can feel it."

His jaw tightened and he nodded. "Let's keep looking."

He slipped around me, moving deeper into the museum. Every time I got close to his side, he moved away. I supposed it was to be expected, though.

A moment later, I spotted a map room. I grabbed Tarron's hand, ignoring his flinch, and pulled him along. "Let's check here."

The room was small and dark, with big wooden cases full of maps. Reproductions, probably, given their age and the fact that we were allowed to sort through them.

It took a few minutes of searching, but finally we found a map of the city from the late medieval period. The lines were faint and the drawing faded, but it revealed endless narrow passages through the ancient buildings.

"This has potential," I said.

As if she'd heard me, my sister's voice whispered out of

the comms charm around my neck. "Mari? Where are you?"

I pressed my fingers to the charm. "Map room. I might be onto something."

"Me too."

"Do we need to come there?"

"No. I don't think so. We'll come to you."

I continued to study the map, but there were so many buildings that it was impossible to tell which might be important enough to contain our ghost. She arrived a few moments later, leaning over the map and pointing to the huge stone wall that ringed the city. "Here."

"The wall?"

"No. Rooms *within* the walls. We saw models of them in the diorama room. Apparently, there are prison cells built right into the city walls."

"Ah, and that's what the abbot said." I nodded. "The ghost would be found within the city walls."

"We interpreted it to mean that he was in one of the buildings contained within the walls." A grin flashed across Tarron's face, and I wished desperately that he'd be well again so I could enjoy his smiles without worrying what was coming after.

The four of us leaned over the massive map, searching the image of the huge circular wall that surrounded the city.

Tarron spotted it first. He pointed to a widened section of the wall that looked like it was filled with bubbles. "Those must be the cells."

"Agreed." I straightened. "Let's check them out."

By the time we made it out of the museum, the streets were full. People bustled between the crowded little buildings, and we had to dodge around them as we hurried up the cobblestone lane. Magic sparked on the air, and tiny pixies flitted about. York was one of the most magical cities in England, and it showed.

It didn't take us long to reach the portion of the city wall where it widened enough to accommodate cells. Stairs led all the way up to the top of the wall so people could walk around the top of it, but I had eyes only for the middle portion.

"I don't see a way to get in."

"Neither do I." Aeri stopped next to me, staring up at the wall.

"Partway up the stairs, there's an alcove into the castle wall," Tarron said.

I moved slightly so I could see it. "Definitely it."

We hurried toward the stairs, and I raced up, taking them two at a time. There was indeed an alcove right by the stairs, with a huge wooden door set deep into it.

A massive metal padlock looked like it hadn't been opened in decades. Centuries, maybe.

"I've got it." Tarron pressed his hand to the metal, which flamed red, then orange. Finally, it melted into a puddle on the stone step.

Tarron pushed open the door, which creaked ominously.

"Perfect for ghosts," Aeri whispered.

I stifled a small laugh, which was probably as much nerves as it was humor.

The hallway within was dark and narrow—and only about six feet deep. It led to another door, which wasn't locked.

A sense of anticipation streaked through me as I approached it. My heart thundered and my skin warmed.

Excitement surged.

What the hell?

I had no idea why I felt this way, but it was unmistakable.

There was something past that door that I *really* wanted to see. I could sense it.

My breathing was harsh by the time I reached the door and pressed my hand to it.

"Mari, slow down," Tarron said. "We don't know what's back there."

I didn't listen. I couldn't.

There was no way to explain what I was feeling. I just *had* to get into that room.

Aeri joined me, moving just as quickly. I swore I could sense her excitement, too.

"Do you feel it?" I asked.

"I do. What the hell is it?"

"I don't know."

Together, we pushed the door open and found ourselves in a small but beautifully decorated cell. A nice bed, a bookshelf, and beautiful art covered the wall.

And just one chair.

The ghost of a man sat upon it.

I stepped into the room, my heartbeat going wild. Aeri pushed in beside me.

He stood.

We stopped.

Holy fates.

It was like looking in the mirror at an older, more masculine version of myself. Or Aeri. The bone structure was the same.

"Holy fates," Aeri said beside me.

Shock lanced me, ice through my veins, followed by fear and joy and every emotion I could name. I'd never seen him before—not in my memory, at least. But it was so obvious that it was him.

"Father?" I asked, my voice whispery.

Aeri squeezed my hand. I swallowed hard.

The man's jaw slackened slightly. "Daughters."

Holy fates, holy fates, holy fates.

My father was the ghost of the Dragon Blood. *That's* why the abbot had looked at me funny.

Tarron came to stand next to me, and Declan joined Aeri.

I was so shocked I could barely process what was happening.

Tears gleamed in my father's eyes, and he looked as shocked as I felt.

"I never meant to leave you," he blurted.

Oh, thank fates. It was a question that I hadn't realized I'd been thinking. But I had been.

"I'm Mari."

"I'm Aeri."

He raised his hands. "I would embrace you if I could."

"What happened?" Aeri asked.

"I was killed shortly after your birth."

"By my mother?" I asked.

"No. I was killed here, in York. But it is a story for another time. I need you to know, however, that I *never* meant to leave you."

I squeezed Aeri's hand tight. I believed him. She glanced at me. From the look in her eyes, she believed him, too.

"You are bound here?" Aeri asked.

He nodded. "Only the magic of this place can keep me on the earthly plane."

"Is it a coincidence that we're looking for the Dragon Bloods and our father is the keeper of their location?" I asked.

"No, indeed not. There are many others that you could have asked. But fate would have you come here, to me."

Of course. When I'd asked my sense of premonition to help me find answers, of course it would lead me to the route that was closest to my heart.

"Come." My father started toward a tapestry on the back wall. He flicked it aside and revealed a hidden door. "We will sit."

"Are you a prisoner here?" Aeri asked.

"Here?" he looked around. "No. These are my chambers, undisturbed by the outside world." He shot Tarron a look. "Until you destroyed the lock."

Tarron inclined his head. "My apologies. I will fix it."

"Thank you. See that you do."

I gestured to Tarron. "This is Tarron, King of the Seelie Fae. And Declan, a Fallen Angel."

My father's keen eyes studied the two men, then he nodded and turned to the door. He opened it and stepped through.

We followed him into another small stone room. In the center sat an ornate round table, dark wood decorated with the heavy carvings that I associated with the medieval period. This room was also lined with tapestries, and I got the impression that my father had never fit into the modern world.

"Are you content here?" I asked.

"Very." He inclined his head. "I chose to stay, to have this task." He hesitated. "So that I might one day see you two."

My throat tightened. In all the misery of the last few months, I hadn't even thought to hope for something like this.

It was a gift.

My father sat, and the rest of us joined him. When he spoke, his voice was heavy. "You are looking for the Dragon Bloods, then."

"Yes," Aeri said. "We have your power."

"Then why do you seek them? Most descendants of the

original dragons never look for them. It's incredibly dangerous."

"We don't have a choice," I said. "My mother has escaped her imprisonment and is coming after Tarron's kingdom. She's already poisoned the Unseelie Court, and the Seelie Court will be next."

"We need to save them both," Tarron said.

I leaned forward. "I believe the only way to do that is to find the Dragon Bloods and request more power. I need to become stronger."

My father frowned. "I'm not sure that is how it works."

"They gave me this power," I insisted. "They can give me more—enough that I can become like her. Strong enough to defeat her."

"She's impossibly strong," my father said. "But becoming like her... I do not think that is the answer."

"I need more strength, though. And we need to heal Tarron."

My father looked at Tarron, then nodded. "The curse on you is strong."

"Can you tell us how to find the Dragon Bloods, then?" I begged. "How do we find the Slate Isles? What are they?"

My father sighed. "The Slate Isles are a series of islands off the coast of Western Scotland, near the little town of Ellenabeich. They are made of the same slate that roofs many of the houses all over the world."

"They're quarry islands?" Tarron asked.

"A few of them are," my father said. "The ones closest to land. They're torn up from the quarrying, but that just makes them better cover for the dragons. Humans believe that the stone is quarried by other humans. When in fact, it's quarried by magic before it's sold on the mainland. But it's the main islands that you are interested in. They are also torn up—but by the activity of the dragons."

"Real dragons?" I'd heard the myths about our origin— that we shared the blood of dragons. But I'd never known —and had no one to ask—what that really meant. *How* did a human get Dragon Blood?

"Yes," my father answered. "Real dragons. Some of them can adopt human form. Perhaps all can, but choose not to. I have had precious few opportunities to visit in my life, and even then, I did not learn all their secrets."

"How do we find them?" Aeri asked.

"There is a portal in the crypts of York Minster. Enter it just before dawn tomorrow, using this." He flicked his hand, and a shiny black flake appeared in it. He passed it across the table to us.

I leaned over to look at it. "A dragon scale?"

"Appropriate, is it not?"

"It is. But what does it do?"

"You'll figure it out."

"What happens when we exit the portal?" Aeri asked.

"You'll need to catch a ride. Find the sleeping stone dragon, and from there, it is up to you. But be sure that you approach the islands with his help—and only during the daylight. The dragons would not take kindly to uninvited visitors in the dark. That's when thieves sneak in, and dragons are notoriously protective of their treasure."

"Will they welcome us?" I asked.

"That is difficult to say," my father said. "They are used to their solitude. But they lend help when it is needed. Not that it is easy to obtain. You must prove yourself."

The seriousness in his voice made me swallow hard. It would not be easy.

"Can we come back and visit you?" Aeri asked.

It was the question I'd had on my mind as well.

He nodded. "I would like that."

Wow. I smiled. "Thanks."

"No, thank you."

We said our goodbyes and left. It was getting dark already.

"We need to find a place to get some sleep." Aeri looked at me. "It'd be better if you saved your powers and didn't transport us back to Magic's Bend."

I nodded.

"I know a place," Tarron said. "An inn. It's old, but charming."

"Lead the way." I took his hand.

He almost pulled away, and from the worried look in his eyes, I understood why.

I gripped him tighter, leaning close to murmur, "I can handle myself."

"Not if your mother gets control of me."

I shivered, but didn't let go. "I can handle that, too."

The inn was close, located down a narrow street right near the massive York Minster cathedral where we would be able to find the portal in the morning. A sign hung out over the door that read *The Guy Fawkes Hotel*.

"Was it really his house?" I asked, thinking of the famous plotter who'd tried to assassinate King James I.

"They say he was born here." Tarron stepped inside the tiny foyer, and I followed him in.

The space opened up to a little pub on the left. The small wooden bar gleamed. Behind the counter, an impressive gin selection shined beneath the lights. A young bartender looked up and smiled. He reminded me of Connor, with his floppy dark hair and T-shirt.

As Tarron approached and arranged for two rooms, Aeri squeezed into the foyer next to me.

"Can you believe that just happened?" she whispered.

"I really can't." I grinned at her. "I'm glad though."

She hugged me. "Me too."

It wasn't just us anymore. Now, we had our father.

Sure, he was a ghost who lived within the medieval prison of York, but I'd take it.

Tarron returned from the bar and held up three keys.

"Three?" I frowned.

"For me." His tone brooked no argument, and I didn't bother. As much as I trusted him, he was right—the false queen and her magic were to be feared. "The staff will bring up dinner to us. We'll sleep, then head out early."

I nodded and followed him up the creaking stairs. Declan and Aeri went into their room, and I followed Tarron into his.

He turned to me, his brow creased. "We're sleeping alone."

"I know. But I can still eat dinner with you."

A small smile tugged at the corner of his lips. "I'd like that."

The room itself was beautiful, with a vaulted ceiling and round windows overlooking a little courtyard filled with tables.

Tarron pulled me toward him. "Are you sure about this?"

"What? Going to see the Dragon Bloods?"

"Yes. And asking them to make you more like your mother. That's your goal, isn't it?"

"To be as powerful as her—yes. Not evil. But I need to be able to fight fire with fire."

"I'm not sure that's the best idea. That seems like it would just create more fire."

"I can control it." I clenched my fists. "And if the Dragon Bloods don't think that is a solution, they'll have another one. I *know* they will."

"You know, or you're desperate?"

"Maybe both." I reached up and held his face. "I'd do anything to save you."

"That's what I'm afraid of."

He was worried I'd risk my life for his.

Of course I would.

I'd risk everything.

"I'm going to try to get in touch with Claire." I drew in a deep breath. "But I need to do it alone."

His brow furrowed.

"She may reveal something about the Resistance location. If the false queen gets control of you—or manages to use you as a spy—I can't risk them."

His jaw tightened. "But you'd risk yourself in my presence?"

"To save you, of course." I shrugged. "It's obviously risky, but this is something I can try to control."

He nodded. "I understand."

There was still a light of pain in his eyes, but he did clearly get it. He'd do the same.

"I'll be in the hall." He left the room and I knelt, reaching into the ether to withdraw my bag of potion bombs. I fished around for the tiny vial of powder that I knew should be floating around the bottom somewhere.

The familiar shape hit my fingertips, and I grabbed it. Quickly, I pulled out the cork and tossed a pinch into the fire.

"Show me Claire."

The flames flickered and danced, and Claire's face appeared. She had a streak of dirt across her cheek, and her dark eyes were weary.

She smiled at the sight of me. "Mari."

"Claire. How are you?"

"Good. We're here in the Unseelie Realm. Luna used your blood and helped us get in. We've made contact with the Resistance."

"And what about the queen?"

"She's up to something, definitely," Claire said. "Just

like your dream said. The Resistance has been keeping an eye on her, and they think she's preparing something. She's really ramped up her efforts in the last twelve hours. A lot more magic is coming from the castle."

"Of course she has."

"When can you get here?" Claire asked. "The sooner the better, I think. She's growing more powerful with every hour that passes."

"Hopefully soon. We've found the Dragon Bloods and are going tomorrow at dawn."

"Good. We're continuing to gather Resistance forces here. Now that you're in the picture, the Unseelie here are more confident in their ability to take on the queen."

"Fates, I hope their faith is well placed."

"It is." Claire smiled. "I'd bet my life on it."

"You are. Just by being there. And I appreciate it more than I can say."

"I like a good adventure. I like revolt even more."

That's what this all was leading to—a legit revolution. "We'll be there soon. Be safe."

Claire disappeared in the fire.

I stood and opened the door. Tarron stood about five yards down the hall, and he turned to me. "Safe to come back?"

"Come on."

I returned to the room, and he joined me, shutting the door behind me. He joined me in front of the fire, where I stood absorbing its warmth.

"I'm really sorry about that," I said.

"It's fine."

"I can tell from your voice that it isn't."

"It's the circumstance, not you." His face soften briefly, right before his lips tightened and his brow furrowed. The energy in the air changed.

"Are you okay?"

"Fine."

But his voice was gruff. His eyes were pinched at the sides, but they were still green. "All right, if you're sure."

"I—" He doubled over, gasping.

I gripped his shoulders. "You're unwell."

"Go." Tarron gasped, his voice ragged. "Mari, get away."

Shit. This wasn't sickness—it was the false queen. I backed away, but he was too fast.

His eyes flashed a brilliant gold, shot through with black. The change came on impossibly fast.

My heart spiked into my throat. "This isn't you, Tarron."

"Of course it's me," he growled.

I backed up toward the wall, my mind racing. The false queen's influence was coursing through Tarron. His eyes gleamed gold and his face was set in harsh lines. Fists formed at his sides.

"Stop it. You're stronger than the curse."

"I *am* the curse." He backed me up against the wall, looming over me.

Oh, shit.

7

TARRON LOOMED OVER ME, CAGING ME IN WITH HIS ARMS. His usual signature, the scent of an autumn day, had been replaced by the reek of brimstone.

"It really isn't you," I whispered.

"Of course it is," he growled.

A shiver of fear raced over me. It was like the man I loved had been replaced by a monster who wore his skin.

He grasped my throat, cutting off my air. I gasped, but all I could do was choke. He tightened his fist.

"Stop," I tried to say, but the words were strangled.

He just tightened his fist more.

Shit.

"You could have been on her side," he hissed.

My vision began to blacken, and terror spiked within me. He wasn't going to stop.

An animal instinct to fight back rose within me. I reached up and punched him in the face, giving it all of my

Dragon Blood strength. His head snapped back, and he grunted.

The fist around my throat loosened briefly, and I gasped in air.

Tarron looked back at me, green flickering in his golden eyes.

"Fight it," I begged raggedly.

He shook his head, his hand loosening at my throat.

"Fight...it."

His eyes turned gold and his fist tightened.

I struck him again, panic beating wildly behind my ribs. His head snapped back again, and when he looked at me, his eyes flickered green. His fist loosened.

"Fight it," I begged.

He tore himself away from me, gasping and leaning over, his hands propped on his knees. "Get away from me."

I backed toward the far wall. "You're stronger than her, Tarron."

He sucked in a harsh breath and stood. His eyes were green once more. "I won't always be able to fight it." His voice was so ragged that it broke my heart. Shadows danced in his eyes. "You can't be near me."

"Yes, I can. Because I'm as strong as you. I can fight this when it happens."

"Can you kill me?" He stalked toward me, intensity in his voice. "Because that's what you need to be willing to do."

Memories of us flashed in my mind—us, kneeling in the Seelie court, the knife in our hands.

I hadn't been able to kill him then. But if I had to... I straightened my shoulders. "Our kingdoms rely on me. Only I can defeat the false queen. So yes, I can do what is necessary."

"Kill me. That is what is necessary if I turn on you again."

My heart twisted. "Yes."

He nodded, his jaw set. His magic sparked briefly, and he conjured a pair of iron manacles that had a very short chain between two wrist loops. He snapped one onto his left wrist, then put his hands behind his back and snapped the other.

I swallowed hard and nodded, hating the sight of him like this, but appreciating it. "Thank you."

He nodded. "Anything for you."

"Keep that in mind if this gets harder. Because I'm going to heal you, no matter what. I don't care if the curse turns you fully to her side. I'm going to drag you along until I can fix you."

"Then we need to find this cure. *Soon.* Because I won't make it much longer."

"We will. I swear it."

"You fight for what you want."

"I fight for what I love." I approached him, my legs shaking from the adrenaline.

He was back with me. His eyes were green once more, his expression familiar. I wasn't going to lose this opportunity.

I stopped in front of him, standing up on my toes to

press a kiss to his mouth. He groaned and dipped his head low, capturing my lips with his own.

My heart thundered as he kissed me. I reached up and wrapped my arms around his neck, pressing my body full length against his.

He shuddered. "I wish I could touch you."

"It's all right. I can touch you." I pushed him back against the bed and climbed on top of him.

He growled and moved beneath me, strong and hard. I pressed myself against him, kissing my way down his neck. I began to pull at his shirt, but with his arms behind his back, it was impossible to get it off.

"Cut it off," he rasped. "I can conjure another."

I drew a dagger from the ether and did as he commanded, slicing the clothes away from his strong chest. Heat welled within me as the clothing fell away, revealing long expanses of smooth skin stretched taut over iron muscles.

I pressed my lips to his chest, and he arched up toward me. I slowed down, determined to enjoy every second. After all, this might be our last night together. I was going to take advantage of it.

The next morning, I woke alone. After an amazing night, Tarron had gone to the other room and barred the door. He'd never once taken off the manacles, which I appreciated as much as I hated.

But damn if I wasn't ready for this to be over.

It didn't take long for me to dress in my fight wear. Before he'd left last night, Tarron had conjured me some fresh socks and underwear, which was so thoughtfully domestic that it made tears prick my eyes.

Dressed, I peeked out the curtains.

Still dark.

Golden street lamps illuminated the courtyard outside, but the tables were empty in the early morning stillness. Perfect timing for us, since our goal was to arrive at the west coast of Scotland at first light and catch our ride to the Slate Isles.

I went to Tarron's room and knocked.

"Come in." His voice filtered through the wood.

I used my key and unlocked the door. He was already awake, though he was still shirtless. As I walked in, he stood. He'd conjured a tight pair of boxer briefs, and damned if he didn't look good.

"How are you?" I asked, warmth suffusing me at the sight of him. He might be cursed to kill me, but when he was himself...

It was all too easy to remember that I loved him.

"Fine," he said. "You?"

"Good as can be expected. Can you conjure the key to those cuffs?"

He frowned.

"You have to," I said. "We need your fighting arm. And we're about to join Declan and Aeri. If you turn, we can take you."

His lips tightened, but he nodded. "All right."

Briefly, his magic flared, and a small silver key appeared on the little table by the bed. I picked it up and went around to stand behind him.

The manacles on his wrists were stained red with blood, and the skin was raw and torn.

I gasped. "What happened?"

"Nothing."

My lips pursed. "You turned in the night, didn't you?"

"I felt her influence, yes."

"But you fought it."

"Barely. Took everything I had."

I swallowed hard, my throat tight.

I was going to kill that bitch.

Quickly, I removed the manacles. He groaned as he moved his stiff arms toward the front.

"Heal yourself," I commanded.

"The pain helps me keep my own mind."

I frowned, but bit back an argument and went to the door. I looked back briefly to see him conjuring clothing.

"We'll fix this, Mari," he said.

I nodded, praying he was right. "We'll meet downstairs in ten minutes."

"See you then."

I went back to my room and fixed my makeup using a quick glamour. At the assigned time, I met Declan and Aeri in the breakfast room next to the lobby. It looked ancient, done up entirely in dark wood that was ornately carved.

Aeri handed me a paper-wrapped sandwich. "Bacon. Not your favorite kind, but bacon all the same."

My stomach grumbled at the savory scent, and I unwrapped it and bit in. The flavor of English bacon and a soft warm bun exploded in my mouth. "This is amazing. Thank you so much."

Tarron arrived a moment later, and Aeri handed him a sandwich. The staff had kindly put together paper cups of coffee for us, and we set out into the dark morning. The streets were empty at this hour, the cobblestones glinting golden under the light of the street lamps.

With all of the people tucked away in their beds, the whole town felt as ancient as it looked. Without people in modern clothing filling the streets, it was easy to think we'd stepped back in time.

Silently, we walked down the street toward the enormous cathedral that sat on the other side of the square.

York Minster was one of the most impressive religious structures that I'd ever seen, the front soaring hundreds of feet in the air. The white stone was carved with endless intricate decorations.

We approached the huge wooden doors, and I pushed one open and entered the silence of the space. Though the doors were unlocked at all hours to allow admittance to anyone who wanted to pray, the pews were all empty. The echoing, empty silence made it clear there was no one inside.

The space was huge, with an enormously high vaulted ceiling. At the other end, the altar stood lonely and quiet.

Enormous flower arrangements scented the air, along with the wax of still-burning endless candles.

"Where do you think the crypt is?" Aeri whispered. Her voice echoed in the silence.

"Likely at the other end," Declan said.

We set off down the quiet aisle, our footsteps silent on the stone. Though there were portals located all over the world that went to Ellenabeich, this was the only one located in a church.

It was the perfect location, however. Protected and hidden deep in the crypts, no one knew it was there except the Dragon Bloods.

At the back right corner of the church, we found a tiny wooden door that was locked with a heavy iron padlock.

"I've got this." Aeri dug into the pocket of her white fight suit and dug out a tiny leather pouch. She pulled out a couple little pins, then knelt before it. Within seconds, she had it unlocked.

Tarron grinned down at me. "Probably better than me melting it."

I nodded. "We're in a church. Respect, and all that."

He nodded.

Aeri stood and opened the door. Cool, dark air billowed out, and I leaned over to look down into the darkened stairwell. "Well, that's appropriately creepy, huh?"

"Definitely." Aeri stepped in, hurrying down the dark stairs.

I followed, with Tarron and Declan bringing up the rear. The steps led deep into the crypts, and by the time we reached the bottom, the temperature had dropped by a substantial degree. I shivered and rubbed my arms.

Tarron joined us at the bottom. His magic flared briefly, and several balls of flame appeared in the air in front of us, floating calmly and revealing an enormous arched space filled with statues and crypts.

"We need to go toward the back," I said, repeating my father's directions.

Quickly, we hurried past the beautifully carved alcoves where York's most powerful and wealthy were buried. This had to be the area that was most commonly visited. But we were headed to the quiet part.

The farther we moved, the more unfinished the crypts appeared. Ornate stone support pillars were replaced by rougher ones. The burial alcoves became fewer and farther between, until finally, we reached the empty alcove that my father had described.

"I think this is it," Tarron said. "Looks just as unimpressive as he said."

I reached into my pocket and withdrew the small, shiny black dragon scale he'd given me. I set it on the ground in the middle of the space, then withdrew a dagger from the ether and spilled a drop of blood on it.

Magic flared, and the air shimmered. A portal formed, sparkling gray.

I stepped forward, but Tarron beat me to it, striding through first. Taking the risk.

Quickly, I followed, stepping out into the biting cold air of Scotland at dawn. Pale gray light filled the morning sky as the sun peeked over the horizon to the east. Wind buffeted me from all directions, pricking my skin with a chill.

We stood on a rocky shore with a steep mountain rising to my right. An iron gray sea lapped at the pebbles on the beach, and in the distance, a little ferry motored to a small black island in the distance.

Tarron joined me. "That has to be the closest of the Slate Islands."

Aeri and Declan joined us.

Aeri nodded to the little ferry. "So that's really not our ride, huh?"

"Nope. Not according to...Dad." I looked at Aeri. "Do we call him Dad?"

"No idea. We should ask him next time we see him."

"Yeah. Let's find that stone dragon. Apparently, he's our ride."

"I guess I've heard of crazier things."

We set off across the rocky beach, looking for a particularly large pile of slate. Loose rock shifted underfoot as we walked, and the mountain loomed overhead.

Tarron stopped in front of a huge pile of black shards of rock. "This has to be it."

I tilted my head and stared, looking for the pattern in the pile of rock. Would it be a real dragon? Or was "stone dragon" a euphemism for a portal? My father hadn't been clear.

"It's worth a try."

"Agreed." Aeri was already dragging a blade from the ether.

I followed suit, calling upon a silver dagger.

"On three?" she asked.

I nodded, and she counted down.

On one, I drew the dagger across my palm and watched the blood well. When enough of the black stuff had pooled in my palm, I turned my hand and let it drip onto the stones, along with Aeri's white blood.

Magic sparked immediately, fierce and violent. It crackled in the air like lightning, bringing with it the smell of ozone.

Tarron's strong arm grabbed me and yanked me back. I stumbled toward him, moving away from the piles of shifting rock.

"Whoa," Aeri breathed from beside me.

Almost faster than I could process, the rock moved upward, forming a huge shape in front of us. Massive rock wings flared wide, and red eyes peered down at us. It towered fifty feet overhead.

I snapped my jaw shut. "A dragon."

Tarron wrapped an arm around my shoulders and pulled me close to his side. "The Dragon Bloods don't do anything in half measures."

The rock dragon raised its head and blew a plume of fire toward the sky. I didn't think it was quite alive—not in the flesh and blood sense. But it was definitely a dragon of some sort.

"Hello." I waved my arm in greeting, but the dragon didn't indicate that it noticed.

"I don't think he's actually alive," Aeri said.

I ran my gaze over the rocks that formed his body. They hadn't transformed into another material—they'd just magically fitted themselves together to form the shape of a dragon.

"Yeah, agreed."

The dragon lowered itself to its front feet and ducked low, stretching out a wing so we could climb aboard.

Gingerly, I stepped onto the stone wing. It stayed sturdy and strong, not collapsing underfoot, so I began to climb up the slope toward the dragon's back.

My heart thundered in my chest, and I forced myself to take deep breaths. Tarron, Aeri, and Declan followed. I found a seat near the dragon's head, straddling its wide back and finding a handhold on one of the rocky spikes.

"Right behind you," Tarron said.

I turned around and spotted him straddling the dragon only a foot behind me. Aeri sat behind him, with Declan last. As soon as we were all seated, the dragon huffed out a blast of flame and launched itself into the air.

"Holy fates!" I laughed, unable to keep the sound in.

The ground fell away below us, and I leaned over to watch the tiny village grow smaller and smaller. The dragon swooped through the cold air, carrying us over the first slate island. Tiny white houses dotted the small island, built in neat rows on patches of green grass that sat atop the black slate.

"There are people down there," Tarron said. "But none are looking up. We must be hidden."

I grinned, watching as the tiny figures walked up and down the street. No doubt they were touring the island, having no idea what was in the air above them.

"This is amazing!" Aeri said.

"Totally!" It was so different than flying with my own wings.

Hell, I was *riding a dragon.*

It was phenomenal. My heart raced like I was running a marathon, and joy surged through me. Despite the disastrous circumstances of our visit to the Dragon Bloods, it was impossible not to feel amazement when riding a dragon across the wavy gray ocean.

The enormous rock beast swept through the air, flying with power and grace. The farther we got from land, the colder and stronger the wind blew. I shivered and drew my jacket tighter around me.

"There's a storm forming!" Declan shouted over the wind. "To the right!"

I looked right, spotting enormous black clouds swirling high in the sky. They moved toward us unnaturally fast, lightning striking within their depths.

"It's coming right for us!" Aeri shouted.

The wind grew stronger, nearly forcing me off the dragon's back. I crouched low, gripping the rocky spikes for support. Thunder boomed as lightning cracked, so close and loud that my ears rang.

The rain hadn't even reached us yet, which was eerie as

hell considering that the lightning struck hard and fast, illuminating the sky with an eerie white glow.

My heart thundered as it neared us.

A huge bolt cracked right at the dragon, striking the very tip of the dragon's wing, blasting off a few dozen shards of slate. The creature faltered, twisting in the air, and gravity pulled at me. I clung harder, squeezing my legs as I tried desperately not to fall.

8

THE MASSIVE STONE DRAGON SHUDDERED AND RIGHTED itself, beating its wings faster to outrun the storm.

It was impossible, though. The lightning struck harder and faster, chasing us across the sky. Fear surged in my chest. I sat upright, about to slice my finger and call upon my Dragon Blood to create some kind of magic to drive the lightning away.

"I've got this!" Tarron shouted. His magic flared bright, and I looked back, spotting him throw out his arm and send a massive gust of air toward the clouds.

It drove them back, but the lightning continued to strike. An enormous white bolt shot right for us. From behind Aeri, Declan's magic flared, and he shot a dagger of golden lightning right at the bolt that was about to hit our dragon.

The Fallen Angel's lightning was more powerful, and it

drove the other away. The dragon swept low on the air, its rock wings flapping powerfully.

Declan and Tarron held off the storm as the dragon powered its way through, struggling against the gale. I clung tight to the beast's back, using all of my strength to stay on as the creature dipped and dived.

Finally, the sky cleared and the lightning faded.

I sagged against the dragon's back. "Thank fates."

"That was close," Tarron said.

"No kidding." I leaned over the dragon's side and looked down, spotting a few black and green islands in the middle of the navy sea. Icy wind whipped my hair back from my face, making my eyes water as I shivered. "I hope we're close."

A screech sounded from the distance, and I looked up. The fluffy white clouds that surrounded us had begun to spin.

"That's not a storm," Aeri shouted.

"It's definitely not natural," Tarron added.

The clouds spun faster and faster, coalescing to form glinting white ice monsters. They were twice as big as a human. Their bodies were angular, more like living icicles than people, and huge crystal wings extended off their backs.

They shot toward us, glittering in the sun like diamonds.

"There are at least six!" Tarron shouted. "With more forming!"

His magic flared, and he shot another massive gust of air at them. The creatures plowed right through it.

I took my bow and arrow from the ether, gripping the dragon's back with my thighs. The creatures shrieked as they flew toward us.

Carefully, I drew back on the string and got a monster in my sight. It was only fifty feet away. I released, watching the arrow fly straight and true.

It slammed into the icy face of the monster, and the head shattered. Shards of ice flew as the creature pinwheeled through the air, plummeting toward the ground.

Tarron hurled a dagger at a monster who was nearly upon us, hitting him right in the head. The icy skull shattered.

Aeri and Tarron joined in, throwing their own weapons at the creatures. I drew another arrow from the ether and sighted it on one of the beasts. It was nearly to me when I released the string. When the head exploded, the ice shards shot toward me. One sliced my cheek, leaving blazing pain in its wake.

The cut burned like fire, and I slapped a hand to my cheek. There was something extra terrible about it. Poison.

"Don't let the ice cut you!" I shouted.

The pain pounded through my body, unnaturally fierce. I sagged, my strength draining out of me. It took everything I had to stay upright on the dragon.

Tarron took out another creature with a well-placed

blast, then reached forward and grabbed me. "Don't let go!"

I clung to the spikes on the dragon's back, but my vision was going dark.

Tarron's other hand gripped my shoulder, and a blast of his healing energy surged into my cheek. I gasped, straightening as strength flowed through my muscles.

"Thanks." My vision cleared just in time to see another ice monster form in the clouds and hurtle toward us.

I drew a dagger from the ether and threw it at the beast. It slammed into its chest, and the creature exploded.

The dragon dived low, zipping below the clouds. I looked up. No icy creatures followed us, thank fates.

"We're nearly there!" Aeri shouted.

I leaned over and looked down, spotting a large island made of black slate interspersed with patches of green grass. Pools of deep blue water gleamed within the island, looking like the slate had been dug out and they'd filled with rainwater.

The dragon flew right for the beach, landing with a clatter on the rounded black pebbles.

I climbed off, my legs still shaky from the adrenaline, and turned to face him. "Thank you."

My friends followed me off. Once they'd disembarked, he bowed his head, then launched himself in the air and returned to the sky.

"This place is amazing," Aeri murmured.

I spun in a circle, taking in the stunning sight. Early morning sun shot across the gray waves, lighting the tips like diamonds. The island itself was a massive mountain of loose slate that spilled down toward the sea. Millions of pieces of angular black rock tumbled down the slopes. At the top, patches of green grass gleamed. Tiny purple flowers clung to wherever they could find a bit of dirt.

A sense of belonging tugged me upward, toward the top of the loose slate mountain.

"Do you feel that?" Aeri asked.

"Totally. We need to go upward."

Together, we set off up the rocky slope. The rubble shifted underfoot, making it hard to climb. Partway up, the only walkable path became a series of steps, and I veered toward those.

"This is convenient." There was a frown in Tarron's voice as he spoke.

Too convenient.

As soon as he'd spoken, rain began to pour. I ducked my head and continued upward. Tarron tapped me on the shoulder, and I turned back. He handed me a rain slicker that he'd conjured.

"Thanks." I put it on.

From behind, I heard Aeri and Declan thank him as well.

I bowed my head and trudged upward. When the stair in front of me disappeared, I nearly missed it, plunging into a deep ravine.

"Watch out!" Tarron grabbed me, yanking me back against his chest.

"That step was just there!" I looked up, spotting the rest

of the stairs disappearing. A gaping crevasse was left in their wake.

You're going to have to prove yourself.

My father's words echoed in my head.

I sliced my hand and dripped my blood onto the ground in front of me.

The stairs reappeared, and I began to climb. As I went, I made sure that the wound continued to drip steadily. Every time a droplet hit the ground, a new stair appeared.

"Let me take over," Aeri said.

"No, I've got it."

"Seriously." She sounded annoyed.

"No, I mean it. I need to prove myself. You've already completed your final transition, but I haven't." She'd faced down a seriously powerful enemy earlier this year, and it'd taken nearly everything she had. Aeri was definitely in her final form.

Me?

Not quite.

But I would be soon.

The rain continued to pour as we climbed. I kept my head down and my senses alert. Exhaustion dragged at my muscles, and cold chilled my skin. By the time we reached the top, my head was woozy from blood loss.

I stepped on the squishy grass at the top, nearly stumbling. The green expanse stretched hundreds of yards in front of us, a flat top to a mountain carved out by the dragons. Huge black buildings perched here and there, each built from the slate that had been quarried right out of the slope that we'd just climbed.

Tarron joined me, wrapping an arm around my waist for support.

"The rain is stopping," Aeri said.

Gray clouds parted to reveal the sun. Overhead, enormous figures swooped through the air.

I craned my neck, squinting. A gasp escaped me.

Dragons.

Real dragons.

They flew with a grace that our stone dragon had lacked. There had to be a dozen of them, swooping between the clouds. The ones that flew lowest were close enough that I could see the colors of their scales.

Red, green, blue, gold. They were all the colors of the rainbow, with differently shaped wings and heads. Magic radiated from them, so powerful that it nearly bowled me over.

"Holy fates," Aeri breathed. "I've never seen anything like it."

"They're amazing." Tarron squeezed me tight. His magic flowed into me, a healing touch that refueled some of my strength.

A gleaming red one swooped toward us, landing with a powerful thud about fifty yards away. Slowly, it folded its glittering red wings against its body, staring at us with eyes that gleamed like black fire.

It walked toward us, graceful despite its size. The long neck tilted down as the creature moved to smell us. I stood stock-still, fear and wonder racing across my skin as the dragon pressed its nose almost to my chest.

The majestic creature inhaled deeply, and I prayed that I passed whatever test this was. One by one, it smelled us.

Aeri caught my eye and gave me a slightly crazed smile. I nodded.

Yep, this was both the coolest and the most terrifying thing I'd ever done.

Finally, the dragon sat back on its haunches. Since it hadn't barbecued us on the spot, I assumed we'd at least partially passed.

What should I say now?

Before I could open my mouth, magic swirled around the dragon. Crimson streaks formed a tornado, and the creature shrank down to the size of a human. Then it transformed into one, becoming a woman of impressive stature.

She towered over me, eight feet tall at least. Her skin gleamed brilliant red, almost like she were made of rubies. When she moved, light flickered across it, highlighting the fine scales that appeared there. Her eyes continued to burn with black flame, set deep within a face that was only partially human. Black hair waved down her back, and a midnight sheath gown of sleek silk completed the effect.

At least this answered the question of how humans had ended up with Dragon Blood—they could transform.

It must be a carefully guarded secret.

"Mordaca. Aerdeca." Her voice vibrated with power, far

deeper than I'd have expected. "Two of our most impressive Dragon Bloods."

"Thank you." Aeri and I spoke the words at the same time.

I gestured to Tarron. "This is Tarron, King of the Seelie Fae." I moved my hand to indicate Declan. "And Declan O'Shea. Fallen Angel."

She inclined her head. "I am Perisea, one of the dragons here."

"A shifter?" Tarron asked.

"No. Not quite. I do not maintain this form for long. But it allows me to speak with you. When I am in dragon form, I do not have the appropriate vocal cords for speaking."

"Thank you for meeting with us," I said. "I know we came uninvited."

"It was your time." Her eyes flicked to Aerdeca. "Though you followed a different path."

"I did."

"Well done." Perisea smiled at both of us. "Come."

She turned and strode across the grass, her midnight gown trailing in the wind. Her crimson skin gleamed as she walked, and I glanced at Aeri, mouthing, *"Wow."*

Aeri nodded, eyes wide.

The four of us followed her toward the massive black stone building that loomed in the distance. As we walked, I kept stealing glances at the dragons above. Over the years, I'd grown used to my power. But I'd also dissociated it from the dragons that had once given it to my ancestors. I'd never seen any of them, so it was easy to forget.

This would not be easy to forget.

We reached the towering stone building, and Perisea led us under a stone archway and into huge courtyard paved in black slate. A massive fountain burbled in the middle, water sparkling under the sunlight. Flowering trees dotted the space, their roots sunk into the ground between the slate. It was a stark place, harshly beautiful in a way that would stick with me forever.

The strangest sense of homecoming flowed over me, along with a heavy sense of fate.

This is meant to be.

Perisea turned and swept her hand out in front of her. Beautiful wooden benches appeared.

"Please, sit." Though low and soft, her voice rang with authority.

We sat, and she took a seat on her own bench. Her gaze met mine. "Why are you here?"

"I need more magic."

"You are a Dragon Blood. You have the ability to make any magic you so desire."

"I tried." I gestured to Tarron. "He is cursed by my mother. She used a type of magic that has no permanent antidote. We have found one that will temporarily hold off the effects, but it is wearing thin. So I attempted to make the magic to cure an incurable curse." My shoulders deflated. "And it didn't work."

"So you want more magic to heal him."

"Yes. And to defeat my mother, the false queen of the Unseelie Fae. She has plans that will cause massive loss of life, and she's insanely powerful. Growing more so by the day. I have many of her magical gifts, but not the strongest ones. I need to learn those so that I can beat her."

Perisea's brow wrinkled. "You wish to become like her."

"Not *like* her, exactly." I shook my head. "She's cruel. Evil. But her magic... I need power like that to defeat her, and I cannot make it as I am right now."

Perisea frowned. "I'm not sure you are approaching this the right way."

My heart thundered. I *needed* this. "My Dragon Blood gives power. It is a source of magic. If I need more, this is the place to come, is it not?"

She nodded, though shadows still gleamed in her eyes. "It is. But you must be worthy."

"I'll do whatever it takes." I looked at Tarron. "I *have* to heal him."

Tarron frowned. "It's more important that we defeat your mother."

"I know you're worried about your people. But we can do both." I looked at Perisea. "Right? He can be cured? If there's any place that could happen, it is here."

My heart raced, desperation fueling it.

"It is." She searched my face, her gaze intense. "You're willing to take the risk? To try to prove yourself worthy?"

"I am."

Her gaze flicked between my three companions. "It will be risky for you as well."

"I accept that," Aeri said.

Tarron and Declan repeated the sentiment.

"Well then." Perisea stood and swept out her arms.

Magic sparked in the air. Anticipation surged through me.

I was dragged into the ether, away from my friends.

A moment later, I appeared on a windswept hillside. The grass under my feet was bright green, and the black, gaping maw of a slate cave rose up in front of me.

I spun in a circle, facing the sky at the edge of the cliff. "Tarron? Aeri?"

They were nowhere to be found. Instead, there was only the sound of whipping wind and the crashing waves, which slammed into the pebble beach about two hundred yards below.

From behind, the cave called to me.

Perisea wasted no time, it seemed.

Skin prickling, I turned.

I could see nothing within—just a faint bit of light that illuminated the black walls.

You must prove yourself worthy.

Perisea's words echoed in my head. Yep—the challenge was definitely in there. The creepy darkness that led deep into the mountain had Dragon Blood written all over it.

I can do this.

Shivering, I drew in a deep breath and stepped into the cave. Immediately, the air warmed. I inhaled deeply, letting it fill my lungs.

The warmth wasn't comforting so much as threatening

—as if it came from fire. The light that illuminated the space was faintly orange, as well.

I forged ahead, shoving aside any fear. If there was fire in here, I'd deal with it. I'd deal with anything to fix what was broken.

The tunnels sloped sharply downward, studded with shards of black slate. Smaller tunnels jutted off of it, but I ignored them. I picked up the pace, jogging downward. The tunnel grew wider as I ran, and small chambers opened up on either side.

Flashes of gold caught my eye, and I peered in as I ran by.

Whoa.

Huge piles of gold sat inside each one—coins, jewelry, goblets, weapons. It had to be millions' worth. I could just imagine the dragons crouching over their horde, spending long nights amongst these piles of treasure.

I'd never been much for gold—not like the FireSouls were. They shared a soul with a dragon, and something about that made them particularly covetous, like their dragon counterparts.

My blood didn't do that to me—normally.

But right now...

My fingers itched.

What I wouldn't give to go roll around on one of those piles. Maybe drag a few bags home with me.

I shook my head, focusing on the tunnel around me. The darkness called from within. Deeper and deeper I ran —and harder and harder the gold pulled.

It felt like a rope wrapped around my middle, yanking me back.

"The gold will solve your problems." Perisea's voice echoed in the cavern, disembodied and strange.

"It won't!" I shouted. But I *felt* it. Perisea was right. This gold was magic.

I faltered, nearly turning into one of the caverns to my left. The glimmering pile drew my eye, and I swore I could see the magic sparkling around it. With a gasp, I forced myself away from it, continuing to run down into the mountain.

It was as if I could feel Tarron and Aeri down there. Their signatures drew me, and I needed to find them.

"It will save them all," Perisea said. "All the Fae."

All?

I swallowed hard.

That was the only thing I really wanted. To save Tarron and all the Fae.

Torn, I turned back to the gold.

Burn appeared at my side, pressing his thorny body against my leg.

I shook my head, jerked out of my obsession. I looked down at the Thorn Wolf. His fiery eyes blazed up at me.

"Thanks, buddy." He gave me so much strength. So much clarity of mind. But... "I think you need to get out of here, pal. I've got to prove myself worthy."

He woofed low.

"I know. But Perisea sent me here alone. I think I have to finish the drill on my own, too."

Understanding seemed to flash in his eyes—or maybe it was my imagination. But he disappeared.

Without Burn at my side, the gold began to pull at me again.

I shook my head and kept running, nearly going to my knees with the force of my desire for it. Not just because it was shiny and pretty—I'd be a liar if I said I didn't like shiny, pretty things—but because it *felt* like it would solve all my problems. Perisea was feeding some kind of magic into it—she had to be.

There was no way gold would solve my problems—even magical gold. There was no magic that it could perform to get me out of this mess.

It would be up to me. *Only me.*

The pull of the gold loosened, as if my realization had freed me.

I powered onward, jogging though the tunnels, ignoring the chambers full of treasure.

Then I heard it.

Screams. Shouts.

Tarron and Aeri.

Shit.

They were in danger.

9

As I RAN THROUGH THE DRAGON TUNNELS DEEP BENEATH THE slate mountain, Tarron's and Aeri's screams echoed up from the depths of the caves.

Was this where they had gone? Had Perisea swept them up and taken them somewhere down here?

It was really them, not some figment of my imagination. I could *feel* it, as if they were close enough to see.

I sprinted forward, determined to reach them.

Prove yourself worthy.

My breath heaved in my lungs as I raced toward them. They needed me.

More loose slate appeared in my path, threatening to trip me up. The ceiling was low, but I called on my wings anyway, flying along the ground. When the slate on the walls began to move, my heart jumped into my throat.

The stones along the side of the tunnel shifted, forming monstrous shapes. Creatures with multiple legs crawled toward me, like giant spiders made of rock. Eyes of flame burned within their heads, and they hissed loudly.

One lunged for me, and I flew upward, darting away as quickly as I could. The creature reached up with one long leg and swiped for me. I dodged.

As I drew my blade from the ether, a second creature leapt for me. It reached out, smashing one of its stone legs into my hip.

Pain flared as I tumbled, barely managing to keep myself airborne.

In the distance, my sister and Tarron screamed.

My heart thundered, fear chilling me.

The monsters converged on me from below, leaping up, determined to keep me from my family.

These bastards are going down.

As I drew my sword from the ether, I spotted a cluster of tiny monsters huddled against the wall.

My jaw slackened.

Babies?

Crap.

I couldn't kill these bastards, even if they were between me and what I loved. No way I could do that. And Tarron and Aeri would never stand for it, anyway.

These creatures were just protecting their young.

I flew as fast as I could, darting around the leaping stone spiders that lashed out with their legs. One of them hit me in the thigh, and pain surged through me. A blow to the chest drove the air from my lungs.

I ignored it, flying as fast as I could through the tunnel, following the screams.

Until they stopped.

Dead silence...

There was just the sound of my breathing.

Shit.

I reached a junction where the tunnel split off into four directions. Panic surged.

Which one?

I could no longer hear Tarron and Aeri.

No, no, no.

Frantic, I looked down each passage, trying to guess where they were. There was nothing but silence.

Misery and anxiety clashed within me. They were hurt. They were in trouble. I could feel it.

And I didn't know how to find them.

Think.

I spun in a circle, searching for any kind of clue. There was nothing but silence.

And then the dark closed in.

The eerie golden light that had filled the space disappeared, and it was just me and the sound of my heaving breaths.

Frustration surged within me until I wanted to cry. This couldn't be happening!

It took everything I had, but I shoved the feeling of helplessness down deep.

This *wasn't* the end.

I sucked in a breath and closed my eyes. I breathed out,

shuddering, and focused on my surroundings. Focused on the feeling of Aeri and Tarron, trying to use my seeker sense to find them.

No matter how hard I tried, it didn't work. Almost like it was blocked.

No way I'd let it stop me. I imagined them and everything I loved about them, everything that they were. We had a connection. I'd use it to find them. This mountain was where I would get new magic, and damned if I wouldn't make it happen.

I drew a knife from the ether and sliced at my wrist, letting blood flow. Not enough that I would pour out all of my blood and create a permanent power—I didn't have time for that—but enough that I could create new magic that would work to find them.

As my blood dripped to the ground below, I imagined being able to sense their location using only the love I felt for them. It was a bond that was stronger than anything, and that was powerful magic in itself.

Slowly, the air began to change. Almost like I could feel vibrations in it. My heart sang along, thundering in my chest. Pulling me forward. Magic sparked through my veins, lighting me up inside.

I could feel them.

I followed the sensation, flying quickly through the dark. My wings brushed the walls a few times, but my senses carried me safely through the tunnels. I flew as fast as I could, not worried about slamming into the stone. Speed was most important, and I knew my power would lead me true.

When light began to shine from a distance, I blinked, focusing my vision. The tunnel gave way to a huge atrium. I tried to speed up, but I was already going as fast as I could, muscles and lungs burning.

When I flew into the enormous cavern, my wings faltered. The magic that made them work faded, and they grew weaker and weaker. I landed in a hard run, taking in the scene before me.

My heart nearly exploded out of my chest. Tarron was separated from Aeri and Declan. They were bound to pillars on separate sides of the massive room, encased behind thick sheets of ice. The ice was so thick that I could barely see them—but the feeling of them was unmistakable. My temporary new magic pulled hard toward them.

They weren't alone, however.

Two massive black beasts lunged for the ice wall, breathing fire to melt it. The creatures were covered in scales and were at least the size of grizzly bears, though they looked like no animal I'd ever seen in real life. Spikes covered their backs, and horns extended up from their heads.

They ignored me entirely, going instead for my family. Their flaming breath melted the ice wall, sending rivulets of water streaming over the ground. Soon, they'd break through and devour them.

I tried to draw a sword from the ether, but nothing came.

Shit.

I was blocked.

Magic sparked in the air, a spell that would keep me from getting what I needed to fight them. And my wings were disabled.

All of my magic was disabled.

What the hell was going on?

I'd just been able to make magic a moment ago.

A test.

This was a test.

I couldn't take on the two monsters without weapons. They were enormous—those fangs and claws would take me out, then they'd get to my family.

No.

Anyway, killing things didn't necessarily prove me worthy. For all I knew, these were Perisea's pets. I needed a better plan. And I had almost no time to figure it out.

I spun in a circle, searching for clues. There had to be *something* here.

The ground looked uneven near Tarron and Aeri. I sprinted toward them, skidding to a stop at a ledge that plunged downward. A pool of crystal blue water glimmered deep within—at least a hundred feet down.

I swallowed hard, staring into the depths.

There was something down there. It gleamed brilliant red, calling to me.

A solution?

Or death?

The water was freezing cold. I could see a gleaming sheet of ice on the top—thin enough that I could break through it, but icy cold all the same. Something huge swam deep in the water, far enough down that I couldn't see the details. It was easily ten times the size of me, though.

If I jumped in that water, I wouldn't survive long. Even if the monster didn't come for me, the cold would. And if I retrieved what I needed from the depths, how was I going to get back out? My wings didn't even work.

I'd have to scale the rock walls, which could be impossible in itself. There were hardly any handholds that I could see.

It was a death trap.

Shit.

I looked back at Tarron and Aeri.

I could fight *one* of those monsters on my own— maybe. Which meant I could save one of them. Only one.

Not an option.

No time for hesitation.

If this was about proving my strength, damned if I was going to wimp out.

I jumped.

Wind whistled by my head, tearing at my hair. My eyes watered and my stomach pitched. The fall was endless.

When I crashed through the thin layer of ice and into the freezing water, all the breath was driven from my throat. My head ached with pain—the ultimate ice-cream headache—and I nearly opened my mouth on a gasp.

I barely managed to keep it shut, trying to get a handle on myself.

Freezing cold made my muscles want to seize up and quit.

Ignore it.

I kicked downward into the depths, opening my eyes and narrowing my vision on the red glow deep in the water. More light came from somewhere else unknown, illuminating the deep pool and revealing huge slate rocks clustered all around. The sea monster was nowhere to be seen, which meant it was probably hiding behind the slate.

When an image flickered at the corner of my vision, panic flared. I looked toward it, my vision distorted by the pressure of the water.

A massive sea monster swam toward me, rage in its black eyes. The blue and green scales sparkled with light, beautiful despite the threat promised by the creature's claws and fangs. The monster was long and graceful, with four legs tipped with webbed toes. Wings extended from the back, but they waved in the water like fins.

A sea dragon.

It pushed effortlessly through the water, charging toward me, darting between me and the golden red orbs at the bottom of the pool.

I swam behind a cluster of rocks, taking cover as my lungs began to burn. Heart pounding, I peeked out from behind the boulders, taking stock of the creature.

Where should I strike it to do the most damage?

I would be lucky to get even one shot, so I'd have to make it work.

Perhaps to the throat, if I could reach it? There looked

to be an area that wasn't covered quite so thickly with scales. Or the eyes? Those were always good. Punching underwater was difficult, so I'd have to maximize my attack.

Behind the dragon, the eggs gleamed invitingly. One of them was transparent, and inside, a silver dagger glowed.

That was my goal.

I knew it like I knew my own name.

I needed that knife.

And this dragon was all that stood between me and it.

So, the neck or the eyes?

The dragon hissed at me, the noise carrying effortlessly through the water.

Get back, it seemed to be saying.

I frowned, mind racing. The cold and oxygen deprivation were making it hard to think.

But this wasn't so different from the challenge with the spiders.

I'm not supposed to kill it.

Suddenly, it was obvious. The threat to Tarron, Aeri, and Declan had gotten me raring to fight. I'd seen only a violent solution to this problem.

But no...

This sea dragon was just protecting its eggs—one of which I wanted to steal. I didn't think the egg with the dagger had an actual baby monster in it, but the sea dragon might not know that.

I was just a threat.

Obviously, I shouldn't try to hurt the dragon. I couldn't

believe I'd even considered it—chalk it up to terror and freezing cold.

It was one of the scariest things I'd ever done, but I swam out from behind my rock. My burning lungs reminded me that I had barely any time left before my air ran out.

My muscles ached from cold as I swam toward the dragon, holding my hand out in a way that I hoped was non-threatening.

The dragon glared at me with dark eyes, clearly unsure of what to make of me.

It hissed again, then moved its head forward just slightly, sniffing.

I tensed, heart going a mile a minute.

Please.

I was flat out of ideas if this didn't work—and I'd also be dragon food.

Tense seconds passed as my lungs burned and my muscles ached. I tried to imagine all of my good intentions, hoping the dragon could sense that I meant no harm.

Finally, the dragon twitched its head, then swam backward.

I nodded my thanks, then swam past. The gold and red eggs called to me, and I pushed myself hard. The regular dragon eggs were crimson bright and shot through with veins of gold. The one that I sought was semitransparent, revealing the dagger within.

I reached for it, carefully avoiding the other eggs. It was shockingly warm to the touch, and I clutched it close to my chest. I gave the dragon one last grateful nod, then kicked toward the surface.

Every inch of me was nearly numb with cold, muscles aching wherever I could actually feel them. My lungs burned from lack of oxygen, and my vision started to go black at the edges.

The surface still looked so far away.

I kicked harder, seeming to go slower with every inch.

Shit.

I wasn't going to make it.

Hot tears smarted my eyes, strange against the otherwise cold water. I struggled upward, fighting the urge to try to suck in air, since there was only cold water to be had.

Help!

I begged the universe, begged the dragon. I didn't know who I begged, but no one came.

It's just me.

Somehow, I found the strength to kick the last twenty meters to the surface. It felt endless, and by the time I reached air and gasped, I was nearly out of my mind with pain.

Immediately, the air surged into my lungs and through my body, giving my numb limbs strength. I swam toward the black rock wall that extended upward, seeming infinitely long.

How the hell was I going to climb that?

I shoved away my doubts and pushed the dragon egg into my shirt. It managed to stay wedged against my stomach.

"Thank fates." The words came out mumbled and rough as I began to scale the black wall. I was so numb that it was nearly impossible to feel my feet or my hands, but I forced myself upward. Handholds were few and far between, but visions of Tarron, Aeri, and Declan—all trapped and at risk—fueled me. It was the strongest motivation there could be, and it propelled me upward.

Halfway up, I tried calling on my wings.

They didn't come.

Damn it.

Frustration surged within me. I was too slow.

Still, I continued. I nearly slipped several times, barely managing to cling on at the last minute. By the time I reached the ledge at the top, I was so tired that I nearly flopped onto my front.

No, don't break the egg.

I scrambled onto the flat, rough surface and knelt, head bent as I grabbed the egg out of my shirt.

The scaly monsters were still attacking the ice walls with their flames. They were nearly through, the ice so thin that I could see Tarron and Aeri's faces.

Shit. Shit. Shit.

Panic threatened to overwhelm me, but I forced it back, bending over the egg to inspect it. There was a tiny latch in the middle, and I flicked it with trembling fingers. The egg popped open, revealing the dagger within.

It was beautifully ornate, silver and gold. I withdrew it, enjoying the warmth on my palm.

"What the hell do I do with it?" I muttered.

A quick glance showed the monsters nearly through the ice wall.

But no.

Just killing them didn't seem right.

I was a Dragon Blood, in the land of the Dragon Bloods, here to create new power.

There was only one thing to do.

I dragged the blade down my wrist, wincing as the pain cut deep. Magic sparked from the silver, and it was clear that this blade was *different.*

It would be the blade that gave me the magic I needed. It would allow me to adopt my mother's power to heal Tarron and defeat her.

Midnight blood poured over my pale skin as I turned to the other wrist, slicing the skin deep. More blood welled, and I sucked in a deep breath as I turned my wrists to the ground and let the warm blood flow over my cold legs.

I forced my magic out with it, pushing every bit of power that I had into the air around me. As weakness stole over me, I gripped the magical blade tight and envisioned the power I needed.

Healing and strength.

My mother's magic had cursed him, so I'd adopt it and use it to cure him. I'd also use it to fight her on even footing.

My vision began to blacken as more and more of my blood flowed onto the slate around me. The magic that rushed out along with it made my soul feel empty.

More power.

I just needed more. Like her. Enough to heal, enough to defeat. Adopting her skills was the only way I could turn back the damage that she had done.

When I was nearly about to fall over, magic sparked on the air. The hilt of the dagger heated in my hand, and the power rushed back into me, filling me up with strength and warmth. Filling me up with magic like hers.

Please work.

10

MAGIC SURGED THROUGH MY VEINS, FILLING ME WITH POWER I'd never had before. Shaking, I stood. The wounds on my arms had healed, and my strength had returned. Magic pulsed within me.

The monsters that menaced my family spun to face me, sniffing the air as their gazes landed on me. They tilted their heads, clearly curious.

Slowly, they prowled toward me. My skin prickled with anticipation, and it took everything I had not to draw a weapon.

No.

Something told me that was a bad idea. I sucked in a breath and waited, trying to slow my racing heart as they moved forward. They were so big that their heads were level with my shoulders. Each one had to weigh at least a thousand pounds, all muscle and deadly claws and teeth.

They stopped right in front of me and sniffed.

My mind raced as I debated whether or not to draw a weapon.

Then, they disappeared.

My shoulders sagged.

Oh, thank fates I'd read the situation correctly.

The cavern was quiet except for the sound of my heaving breaths. I stood alone with my family, power coursing through me. The ice walls still encased Tarron and Aeri, but they were thinner than they had been.

I rubbed my hands together. Time for a little magic.

I called upon my new power and thrust out my hands, envisioning blasting golden light that the false queen had conjured. Surely it could blow away these walls.

Nothing came.

Frustration surged inside me.

I tried again.

Still, nothing came.

What the hell?

I had magic—I could feel it. But not the power that I'd asked for, it seemed.

Fear chilled me, followed closely by anger. Had this really not worked?

I called upon an ax from the ether and gripped the wooden handle tight. The ice fortress that surrounded Aeri and Declan was closer to me, so I charged toward them, attacking the wall that stood between us.

Rage surged as I hacked at the ice. Sweat poured down my back as I gave it everything I had—the rage that I couldn't do the job, the rage that I didn't know where to go from here. It coursed through me like fire, and I turned it toward the ice, hacking at it until I could reach Aeri.

Finally, the last shards broke free. I scrambled through the hole and stumbled toward her. She and Declan were tied to a post, both slumped and unconscious.

"Aeri!" I called a knife from the ether and sliced at the ropes that bound her.

She twitched. "Mari!"

I cut the last of the rope free, and she stumbled forward, Declan at her side.

Quickly, I ran around to face her and threw my arms around her. "You're okay!"

She hugged me tight, then pulled back, her gaze confused. "Yeah. I blacked out. Now...I'm here?"

"I'll explain in a minute."

I climbed back through the hole in the rapidly melting ice wall and sprinted to Tarron. Again, I conjured the ax. Rage still drove my motions. Even worse, there was uncertainty. I hadn't done what I'd come here to do. I had new power—I could feel it—but not what I'd expected. Not all that I wanted.

Please let the healing work.

Something had changed in me, and I prayed that it would be the ability to heal Tarron.

My lungs heaved as I smashed my ax against the ice, the force of the blows singing up my arms. Finally, I hacked through the last of the ice, forming a hole big enough to climb through. I scrambled inside, cutting myself on shards of ice. Pain shot through my arm where the ice had slashed me, but I ignored it.

Like Aeri and Declan, Tarron was slumped against his bindings.

"Tarron!"

His head jerked up and his eyes flared gold and black.

Shit.

"You." He hissed, thrashing against his bindings. His muscles bulged and his face turned red as he fought to reach me.

I gripped his shoulders and shook him. "Tarron! I know you're in there!"

"I'm coming for you. *She's* coming for you."

That bitch. I couldn't take it anymore. She'd been hounding me since this began, and I was going to take her out. I didn't care that I didn't have the magic she did. I was going to end her.

But first, I was going to heal Tarron, damn it.

I wouldn't fail at that. Couldn't.

I sucked in a deep breath and gripped his shoulders tightly. My new magic bubbled up inside me, and I fed it into him. "I'm going to find this poison and drive it out of you."

"The hell you will," he growled.

My magic connected with his, and suddenly, I could feel the curse that was inside him. Like black ink spilled over his soul, it polluted him. The curse took away the goodness and replaced it with the false queen's evil rage.

I forced my own magic toward it. The healing power

connected to his soul—something I'd never been able to do before. Maybe it was a version of my mother's magic or maybe it was something entirely new.

But it's working.

Determination and energy flowed through me, and I pushed them into him. No way I was stopping this until it was done, even if it killed me.

And I'd finish in time. We didn't have long until the final battle came, and Tarron would be on my side fully. I might not have all the magic I needed to defeat her and survive the battle—but damned if I'd give up.

As my magic stamped out the evil that had been painted onto his soul, the gold began to fade from Tarron's eyes. The black streaks receded, and his struggles slowed.

"What are you doing?" His voice was still rough with anger, but confusion flowed between the words.

"Healing you." My heart pounded. The darkness was almost gone. "Bringing you back."

He jerked away halfheartedly, but the bindings kept him in place.

Finally, I drove the last of the darkness from his soul.

He blinked, his eyes totally green once more. "Mari?"

"Tarron!" I threw my arms around his neck and hugged tight. "Do you feel her anymore?"

"No. She's gone."

I pulled back, joy surging through me. I might have failed at part of this—but not all of it, thank fates.

I'd *healed* him.

Ecstatic, I pressed my lips to his and kissed him with

everything I had. He groaned and kissed me back, so skilled that he swept my mind away.

Someone cleared their throat behind me, and I groaned, pulling back.

Tarron gave me a half smile, relief on his face. "Your sister wants you."

I turned, exhaustion pulling at my muscles. I'd used so much magic, and I could feel it. Standing on the other side of the ice wall with her head peeking through the hole was Aeri.

She grinned at me. "Perisea is here to see you."

Shit. I turned back to Tarron. "We'll finish this later."

"Damned straight we will."

I hurried around behind him, using a dagger to saw away at the bindings that lashed him to the post.

He freed himself and shook out his arms, then turned to me. "How'd we get in here?"

"Perisea. You remember nothing?"

"I blacked out."

"Aeri said the same." I climbed back through the hole in the ice and found Perisea waiting for me.

Unlike before, she was in her dragon form. Awe filled me at the sight of her. She was incredible. Her crimson scales glinted in the light, and her black claws gleamed like onyx. Ebony eyes watched me carefully.

I stood still under her inspection, hoping I was passing.

Finally, magic swirled around her, and she transformed to her semi-human body.

She sauntered toward me, all grace and power. "You've completed the tasks."

"Have I?" I asked as she stopped in front of me. "Because I don't have everything I came for."

She shrugged elegantly. "My Arachanaliths report that you didn't kill them or their young. And the Hydrera, the water dragon, allowed you to pass. So it seems that you proved yourself worthy." Her gaze moved to Tarron. "And he appears to be healed."

I looked back at Tarron, who stood a few feet behind me, clearly healthy again. I hadn't realized that he'd looked different before—and he hadn't, not really. But he'd *felt* different. Like his aura had been off.

That difference was gone now, and he was entirely back to himself. It soothed the not-so-low-level anxiety that I'd been harboring.

I turned back to Perisea. "You're right. I did heal him. And that was the most important thing." I ignored his gruff noise of disapproval. "But I'd hoped to get the same crazy golden magic that the false queen has. The speed and power of that is something we can't possibly beat. We've tried."

"Have you tried everything?"

"Yes!" I wanted to shout the words, but I managed to keep my tone at a reasonable decibel. Barely. "We've tried everything, and I'm still not as strong as she is."

"Perhaps you're approaching this the wrong way." Perisea tilted her head. "Perhaps you need to remember who you are."

"What does that mean?"

A thunderous boom shook the cavern. Slate chips rained from the ceiling, and I staggered, covering my head. Even Perisea stumbled.

Her black eyes widened as they met mine. "She comes."

"What?"

Before Perisea could answer, a white light flashed in the middle of the cavern.

The false queen appeared, tall and powerful, her lacy black dress looking like it was made of chips of black glass strung together with threads.

"Daughter." She strode toward me, her hair in an elaborate updo that was threaded through with spikes. "I have been looking for you."

"Oh, have you?" Fear thrummed through me as I drew my sword and shield from the ether. I wasn't strong enough to fight her—I could feel the strength of her power wafting toward me. If she struck out, I was going down. Deep in my soul, I knew that my ability to reflect magic would no longer work against her. The power imbalance was too obvious. But maybe the shield could help a bit. At the very least, I needed to draw her attention from the others.

"Of course." Her gaze flicked to Aeri, who stood about twenty feet to my left. "Both of you are integral to my plan."

"And what is that?" I asked, stalling for time while I hoped that Perisea might transform into a dragon and fry her ass with some fire. That might be the only thing that could defeat this bitch.

She laughed. "I couldn't possibly tell you, though I will say that your blood—both pure and tainted—will come in very handy. But rather than explain, I think it's better that I just *take* you."

She raised her hand, magic sparking around her.

I ducked behind my shield.

"You shall not!" Perisea roared. She thrust out her palm and shot a blast of fiery magic at the false queen. It was so bright that it blinded me, but I heard the false queen's scream.

Frantic, I blinked, trying to clear my vision. I caught sight of the false queen disappearing, the hem of her black dress the last thing to go.

She was gone.

"Is everyone okay?" I spun in a circle, searching for my family and Perisea.

Aeri, Tarron, and Declan looked fine. Perisea, on the other hand...

She was on her knees, her crimson form duller than before. She no longer sparkled under the light, and her eyes were dimmed.

"Perisea!" I sprinted toward her and knelt at her side, gripping her arms to support her.

"Thank you." She took the help gratefully, her voice hoarse.

"No, thank you." I looked at the spot where the false

queen had once been. "Somehow, she made it here, but you stopped her."

She coughed and nodded. "That kind of magic is very powerful, but it drains me."

Aeri knelt at our side. "Will you be all right?"

"Eventually, I hope."

I called upon my healing magic, hoping that it might work here. I didn't fully understand it yet—it was somehow related to the soul and capable of things I didn't understand. But I had to try.

Carefully, I fed the healing energy into her. Tarron joined us, kneeling at my side.

He caught Perisea's eye and hovered his hands over her shoulders. "May I?"

She nodded. "Though I doubt you can fix me."

"We can try." He gently laid his hands upon her shoulders and fed his magic into her. I felt his healing energy combine with mine, and slowly, Perisea's brightness began to return.

As my magic flowed into her, I grew weaker. My limbs started to feel heavy and my mind to slow. Next to me, Tarron seemed to grow dimmer as well, as if the light of health was fading from his skin.

Perisea pulled back, breaking our hold on her. "Stop. You cannot give me too much."

"But you could die." I reached for her.

She dodged, coughing. "I will not. I will heal." Her gaze moved to the spot where the false queen had been. "And you must retain your strength to fight her. She is most powerful."

"An understatement." Despair filled me. "I can feel that I didn't get what I needed to fight her. She is still too powerful."

"Remember who you are." Perisea stared hard into my eyes, as if trying to will me to understand. Stars sparkled in her dark eyes, a strange knowledge lingering there. "Now go. I was able to see what the false queen is planning. What she has accomplished. And it is not good. She has infiltrated your realm." Her gaze moved to Tarron. "Taken over the minds of some of your subjects. You do not have long before she has taken all of them. Her power grows with every conquest."

Oh.

Suddenly her growing power made sense.

"What is she planning?" Aeri asked.

"As she said, something with the two of you. Your blood." She looked at Aeri. "Pure dragon blood." Her gaze moved to mine. "Tainted."

I frowned, not liking that term.

Before I could argue, she said, "You have something in your possession that will help. Aranthian Crystal."

I frowned. "But it doesn't freeze the false queen."

"Still, it will be useful. In the moment, you will know." She flicked her hand. "That is the most I can tell you. Now go. And be victorious."

The ether sucked me in, spinning me through space. I reached out, trying to stop myself from being dragged away. But it was too late. I was swept into the ether and thrust out onto the street in front of my house.

The last thing I heard was the echoing voice of Perisea, "Have faith. And remember who you are."

The words floated eerily in the air, fading quickly away.

Nighttime had fallen in Darklane, and the street lamps shed a golden glow over the cobblestones. I spun in a circle, taking in the quiet, empty street.

Tarron appeared next to me, then Aeri and Declan.

"What the hell just happened back there?" Tarron asked. "The false queen actually arrived there, didn't she? It wasn't just an illusion."

"Yeah." Horror opened a hole in my chest. "She's so powerful she was able to transport into that stronghold."

"Do you believe Perisea?" Aeri asked Tarron. "That the false queen has infiltrated your realm?"

"I will check." He raised his wrist to his lips and spoke into his comms charm. "Luna? Are you there?"

"King Tarron!" Relief sounded in Luna's voice. "We've been trying to reach you. The Unseelie queen has somehow gotten her hooks into our court. Her magic has polluted the minds of some of your subjects."

Shit. So it was true. And it must have happened while he was unconscious in the dragons' slate caverns.

"How many?" he asked.

"Twenty percent, maybe. And counting. It's worse in the Unseelie Realm. Everyone who is not in the Resistance is on her side. With the way her strength is growing, we don't have much longer."

I looked between my companions, dread unfurling within me. I'd gotten as much magic as I was going to get for this battle.

I drew in a deep breath. "This is as good as it's going to get. It's time to join the Resistance."

Aeri's jaw firmed. "You're stronger than you think you are, Mari. I know you didn't get what you went for—not all of it, at least—but Perisea is right. There must be another way."

"What is it, then?" I asked, desperation fueling me.

"You'll find it." Aeri gripped my arm, and I could feel her trying to feed a sense of comfort into me. "But until then, I've got your back. We all do."

"And we all need to head to the Unseelie Realm." Declan looked at his watch. "We've about an hour until the sun rises there. The portal will open then."

I nodded, driving back the fear. It was time to fight.

Tarron nodded. "I must visit my realm, if only briefly. I need to gather the rest of the palace guard. We'll bring troops to the Unseelie realm."

I nodded. "I need to collect some things from my house. We'll meet you at Puck's Glen."

He nodded, then strode toward me. As he gripped my arms and pulled me to him, Aeri and Declan strode up the stairs to our house, giving us space.

"You saved me." His green eyes met mine. "Thank you, Mari."

I nodded, swallowing hard. My throat tightened as I spoke. "I'm just so glad it worked."

"I had faith in you."

"Otherwise you wouldn't have come along." He'd have locked himself away if he thought he were an unsalvageable risk to me or his people.

"Yes." He pressed a kiss to my lips, an urgency in him that I had never felt before. I fell into this kiss, wishing it could last forever. Finally, he pulled back, his gaze intense. "And if we survive what is to come, I want to spend a life with you."

My jaw slackened. "Really?"

"You're surprised?"

Given the depth of feeling that surged within me, well... "No, actually. I love you, Tarron. More than I'll ever love anyone."

He pressed one more kiss to my lips, then pulled back. "Good. I will see you at Puck's Glen in thirty minutes."

I nodded, savoring the sight of him before he disappeared.

Quickly, I turned and raced up the stairs to join Aeri and Declan. I could hear them in her apartment, and I headed to mine. As fast as I could, I changed clothes and repacked my potions bag. I checked to make sure that the Aranthian Crystal was still in there, and was grateful to see that it was. I didn't know how exactly we'd use it against the false queen, but Perisea had been clear.

Anyway, as strong as the false queen was, we were going to need all the weapons we could get.

THIRTY MINUTES LATER, WE MET TARRON AND HIS ARMY IN the clearing at Puck's Glen. There had to be at least fifty Seelie Fae, all armed to the teeth. Serious expressions set their features into stern lines, and their clothing was meant for battle. Simple, with chain mail and leather armor.

I strode to Tarron. "Ready?"

"Ready. More of my troops are in the Unseelie realm with the Resistance. More will come once we know the lay of the land."

I nodded, then turned to the circle of rowan trees that surrounded us. We'd explored this glen before and found that each tree was marked with a knot of wood labeled with a number written in the Fae language. Once I found number one, it was easy to remember the order.

"Sun is coming up." Tarron pointed to the glow on the horizon.

I could feel it in my bones, my Fae power announcing its arrival.

As the rays of light began to shoot through the sky, I sliced my fingertip with my sharp thumbnail and swiped my black blood over the first tree knot. I moved from one tree to the next, going in order, until I'd rubbed my blood on each of the thirteen trees. Last, I moved to the huge flat stone in the middle of the clearing.

Tarron joined me. As I spilled my blood on the stone, he began to chant, reciting the Fae words carved in the stone. Magic sparked on the air, and I stood, stepping back.

Silver branches appeared, forming an archway. Dozens of golden apples dripped from the boughs, magic sparking from them.

Tarron turned to his men, his voice ringing with authority. "Troop leaders, each take an apple as you enter. On the other side, it will create a portal if you need to leave the Unseelie realm."

The men nodded their understanding, and Tarron turned back to me. "Ready?"

"Ready." I drew my sword and shield from the ether and turned to the archway, stepping through without hesitation. The ether sucked me in and spun me through space. When it spat me out on the other side, the sun shined brightly through the trees, an odd welcome to the creepy forest that reeked of the false queen's magic.

Such a strange combo.

I moved into the clearing, blade raised as I searched for Unseelie guards.

Tarron appeared next to me, followed by Aeri and Declan.

All three assumed fighting stances as they fanned out.

"No one here," I murmured. "Too good to be true."

A tall Fae stepped out from behind a tree about twenty feet away. "Depends on which side you're on."

His dark hair and sharp features were distinctly Unseelie, but his eyes appeared to be clear of the false queen's influence.

"Are you with the Resistance?" I didn't lower my sword.

"I am." His gaze traveled over me. "And you are our missing true queen."

"That I am." Though I didn't like the sound of it, I kept my mouth shut on that point. I searched the trees around him. "Where is Brielle, the Resistance leader? Or Claire, Connor? Luna, the Seelie Fae warrior?"

The Fae raised his wrist to his lips and spoke softly into the charm. "They'll be here in just a moment."

The tension didn't fade from my shoulders as I waited. We were on enemy ground and we would be until I took out the false queen. It would never be safe. "Where are the Unseelie guards? The false queen's warriors?"

"We've driven them back from this turf." His gaze flicked proudly around the clearing. "As she grows stronger, so, too, do we."

"More warriors?" Tarron asked. "More supplies?"

"Both, thanks to the true queen." He nodded at me. "And thanks to you. Your warrior Luna brought four dozen warriors with her."

"The rest will come, once we are assured that you are who you say you are," Tarron said.

The Fae grinned. "I am."

A moment later, three figures hurried into the clearing.

Claire, Connor, and Luna. All looked tired but glad to see us.

"Mari!" Claire said, her gaze flicking to Tarron. "How did it go?"

"Well enough," I said.

Tarron stepped forward. "Mari has healed me."

"Though I'm not as strong as I'd hoped to be." Worry tugged at me. The feeling of not being enough, if I were honest. No one needed to hear the true queen say that out loud, though. "But we're out of time, I hear."

Claire's eyes turned shadowed. "We're definitely out of time. The false queen needs to be stopped—now."

"Then we need a plan." I turned to Tarron. "I'd say it's safe to bring the rest of your troops through."

He nodded. "I'll be back."

"I'll lead you to the camp once they've arrived," the Fae guard said.

Tarron nodded. "Thank you."

"Come on." Claire gestured for us to follow. "We'll lead you back."

Luna stayed back with Tarron, while Aeri, Declan, and I went with Connor and Claire. We strode down the forest path as a small group, our footsteps quiet on the leaves.

Claire leaned close to talk in hushed tones. "The Resistance has grown, but we need you."

"Do you know what the false queen is up to, exactly?"

"We have a guess, and the beginnings of a plan."

"Good." I looked around, tension pulling at my shoulders. "This place is really safe?"

"This section of the forest, yes. The Resistance cleared it of the queen's minions and placed powerful spells on it to protect it. But they won't last forever."

"No, that kind of magic is hard to maintain."

A few minutes later, we reached the same camp we'd visited last time. It was larger now, with more hammocks hung between the trees. The bird's-nest style houses had multiplied as well, dotted here and there in the branches. Hundreds of faerie lights sparkled between the branches. A fire burned in the middle of the clearing, with several Fae hard at work on some kind of breakfast they stirred in one huge pot.

Hundreds of pairs of eyes turned to look at us, and I spotted the old woman who'd taken us in her carriage into the castle on the last visit. She gave me an assessing look, and I hoped I lived up to expectation.

Despite all the new faces, I only had eyes for my friends.

I spotted the three FireSouls sitting at a table with Brielle, the leader of the Resistance. The Fae woman was small, with the trademark dark hair and luminous skin of the Unseelie.

Cass, Del, and Nix all turned to face us. My heart leapt at the sight of my friends.

They rose and hurried to us, Brielle at their side.

I hugged each of the FireSouls in turn. "Thank you for coming."

"Of course." Cass grinned. "We had a nap and are ready to go again."

I smiled. "If that's all it takes."

"Were you successful?" Del asked. "How is Tarron?"

"I healed him, but I didn't get the magic I'd been hoping for." I said the words quickly, wanting to spit them out.

Nix shrugged. "Between all of us, I'm sure we can manage."

She wasn't wrong—as a group, we were immensely powerful. If we could manipulate the battle so all of us faced the false queen at once, we might have a shot. It was just getting the battle to that point that I was worried about.

Brielle's gaze flicked to the forest behind me. "I see you've brought reinforcements."

I turned to see Tarron leading the group of fifty Seelie Fae into the camp. "He'll bring more if we need them."

Brielle nodded. "We need our plan, first. Stealth may be more important than numbers."

"What do you know so far?"

"Let's have a seat and discuss it." Brielle walked toward the wooden table where they'd been sitting when we'd first arrived.

Tarron turned his men over to Luna, who set off to get everyone sorted. He joined us, and we all sat at the rough wooden table.

Brielle leaned forward, her gaze intense. "We've been told that you have an Aranthian Crystal."

I nodded. "I had two. I tried to use one on the false queen, but it didn't work."

"No, she's too powerful now." Brielle spit on the ground, a distinctly un-Fae gesture. "But our reconnaissance suggests that she has a source of power that helps her maintain her mind control over the people of this realm."

My mind flashed back. "Like the dark crystal that she implanted into the Seelie court?"

"The theory is the same, yes." Brielle grinned. "You're quite clever, for a future queen."

The way she said it suggested that she didn't like the idea of me being the future queen, and hope surged. But first, we needed to figure out our plan.

Tarron seemed to agree, because he leaned forward. "So we need to destroy this crystal to destroy her hold on the people."

"It's not quite so simple." Brielle raised her hand and ticked off her points as she made them. "First, it's not a crystal. It's a well of power that is vital to all of the Unseelie. We cannot destroy it, or we will destroy much of the magic that keeps this place running."

"Oh, that makes this complicated." I frowned, remembering what Perisea had said. "Hang on. Could we use the Aranthian Crystal to freeze the well of power and weaken her?"

Brielle grinned widely. "Yes. If we can use it to freeze

the well, it will temporarily disrupt her hold on the minds of the Fae here."

"Which would cut off its power to her," Tarron said.

"Giving us a chance to hopefully defeat her." Hope surged in my chest. Maybe I didn't need to be as strong as her.

"Exactly," Brielle said. "Once she is destroyed, her magic will fade from the well, and everything will return to normal."

"We just need to get to the well," Cass said. "Then get to her."

"And that's the hard part," Claire said. "We've been trying to perform some recon, and it's going to be difficult."

"But with our increased troops, we stand a chance," Brielle said. "Although we think she has something else planned. We don't know what, exactly. But she's moving towards completion."

"How can you tell?" Tarron asked.

"Increased magic coming from the palace. It's really ramping up."

"She wants me and my sister," I said. "For our blood."

Brielle nodded. "Queen's blood."

"No." I shook my head. "Dragon Blood. I think that's what she wants."

Brielle winced. "She'll be too powerful with that. You cannot be captured."

"We won't be."

Brielle frowned. "Hard to guarantee."

"Isn't everything?"

"You're brave, I'll give you that," Brielle said. "Won't be so bad, for a queen."

Aeri shot me a loaded look.

"About that," I said. "I'm not qualified to be queen."

"Your mother isn't either," Brielle said.

"Exactly." I gave a wry grin. "I won't be as bad as her. No one could be. But being ruler means making important decisions that I'm not equipped to make. Nor do I want to make them."

"You don't want to be responsible for the lives and well-being of hundreds of Unseelie Fae?" Brielle asked.

"Frankly, no." I looked around, taking in all of the faces watching me. "I want to be here. I want to overthrow the false queen and end her reign of terror. I want to get to know my own kind. But I don't need to pick up the mantle when she is done. There's no reason I should be ruler. I think you could do that."

"Me?" Brielle asked, frowning.

"All of you." I gestured to the group. "Why not give democracy a try?"

"We're a monarchy," Brielle said. "It's written into our lore. Into our magic."

I shrugged. "So change it."

"We *can't*."

I shifted, not liking where this was going. But there had to be a way around it. "Okay then, I'll be queen, but in name only. I'll wear the crown, do a ceremony or two. Whatever it takes to follow the traditions. But governance and rule of law will fall to the people."

Brielle frowned, but interest glinted in her eyes. "You'd agree to that?"

I arched a brow. "Agree to it? Of course. I get a crown, a title, probably the nicest room in the castle. But I also have no responsibility besides the occasional party."

"Not a fan of responsibility, huh?" Brielle asked.

"On the contrary, I'm quite a fan. But I have plenty of responsibilities back on earth. A whole life that I want to keep living. A job that I'm good at." I was a freaking demon slayer, for fate's sake, even though I'd been seriously neglecting my duties. I didn't want to just quit that. Or my Blood Sorcery business. I loved both. They were *me.* "But you know what you need here in the Unseelie Court. What kind of lives you want to live and what the problems are. Therefore, I think you all should make the rules."

Brielle grinned. "I think I'm going to like you, Your Highness."

I smiled. "I can't say I hate the title. But that's as far as it goes. You all,"—I pointed to the whole crowd—"you need to find a way to make the decisions. Have a proper government that doesn't involve a crazy despot."

Brielle nodded. "First we need to defeat the false queen."

"We can do that," I said. And we could. I truly believed that we were going to take her down.

I was just less sure about whether or not I was going to survive it.

12

WE NEEDED A PLAN TO DEFEAT THE FALSE QUEEN, AND IT ALL seemed to revolve around the well of power.

I leaned toward Brielle. "Do you know how to find the well of power?"

"That's the problem." She scowled. "It's hidden."

"You haven't found it, then?" Tarron asked.

"We have not. We've looked. Set all our best people to it —even the FireSouls, now that they are here. But it is in a heavily protected part of the kingdom—one that is hidden from us."

"Is there a backup plan?" I asked.

Brielle pointed to me. "You."

"*I'm* the backup plan?"

"We hope so. We believe that you might be able to sense the well more easily than we can, given that you are of royal blood. It is hidden from the rest of us."

"This royal blood thing really is a big deal to the Unseelie, huh?"

"Yes. I wouldn't be opposed to abolishing the monarchy entirely—no offense intended—if it weren't for the fact that the magic of the royal family is key to this place. It is built into the fiber of the earth."

Talk about responsibility. I repressed a shudder and focused on the task at hand. "I'll find the well of power and I'll deploy the Aranthian Crystal. Once she's weakened, we can fight her."

"That might take an army," Brielle said. "She's so powerful."

"We'll face that when it comes," I said. "First, I'll take out the well."

Brielle nodded. "You need to go undercover. It's deep in enemy territory. Behind the palace, we think. In the royal grove."

"Like the royal grove in the Seelie Kingdom?" I asked. "The same one where the false queen planted the crystal obelisk?"

"Not quite." She looked at Tarron. "That place is relatively stable, correct? A forest full of big trees that don't necessarily change?"

He nodded. "It's just trees. No changes."

"Well, this place changes. It modifies to suit each ruler, reflecting their personality."

I grimaced. "So you're saying it's going to be hell."

"We think so, yes."

"Great."

Tarron shifted. "Can't say I'm surprised."

"Indeed not." Brielle leaned forward. "To even attempt to find it, you're going to have to be invisible. And you should search from the air. Easier to hide you so far from the eyes that might see you."

"You can use my ghost suit," Aeri said.

I nodded gratefully at her.

"Not just invisible to the eye, which we can do with a potion," Brielle said. "We must hide your magical signature from detection. Completely. Not just repress it like you normally do, but make it seem like it doesn't exist at all. While allowing you to still use your magic."

Tarron made a low noise in his throat. "Sounds impossible."

"It was, until the Unseelie Hag joined us," Brielle said. "She's a powerful witch who had been living undercover in the castle until the false queen's influence grew too strong. She's fled to the forest to join us, and she has the magic to block your presence from the charms that would sense you."

"Let's go immediately," I said. "How many can we bring?"

"Just two, I think," Brielle said. "The Hag said that she has very little of the potion required to hide you."

"I'll go," Tarron said.

I met his gaze. "Thank you."

Brielle stood. "Come. I'll take you to The Hag."

We joined her, and she led us through the camp and into the forest.

Aeri hugged me on the way out. "Be safe."

I hugged her back. "I'll see you soon."

She nodded and joined Declan, who stayed behind with the rest to start making plans to launch an attack on the false queen. The exact nature of the final battle would depend on if I could destroy the well of power on my own, but we would need as much backup as we could get in case the fight would be a big one.

Of course it will be a big one.

I hurried to keep up with Brielle, who moved through the forest with the graceful swiftness of a doe. "She lives outside of the camp? Isn't that dangerous?"

"She refuses any other accommodation." Brielle shrugged. "The Hag is a weirdo."

After a few minutes, we came upon a strange dwelling made of trees that had bent over at the trunks to form a ceiling with their branches. An arched doorway led into the dark interior, and Brielle gestured forward. "I told her to expect you."

I nodded and hurried forward with Tarron. A strange scent wafted from the door—spicy and delicious and gross at the same time. *Ugh.*

Together, we stopped at the darkened doorway. There was no actual door, but the interior was so dark that it was impossible to see inside.

"Um, Hag? Hello?" I called.

"It is Mordaca, the true queen, and Tarron, King of the Seelie Fae," Tarron said.

I nudged him with my arm. "Smart. Better to introduce ourselves."

A low voice echoed from within, carrying with it the distinct sound of a smoker's rasp. "Come in, come in."

I hurried in, anticipation and nerves making me jumpy.

The woman who stood over the cauldron at the fire was *definitely* not what I'd expected. For one, she was drop-dead gorgeous. She was probably somewhere in her seventies from the look of the fine lines around her eyes, but she was one of the most beautiful, graceful women I'd ever seen.

Slender and tall, her dark hair was threaded through with silver that glittered like diamonds. Her green eyes were unusual for an Unseelie Fae, but they contained a darkness that was riveting. Her black gown revealed the figure of a supermodel, and she moved toward us with the grace of the angels.

"*You're* The Hag?" I asked.

"Indeed." She smiled, her blood red lips parting to reveal perfect white teeth.

"The name is an interesting choice." I couldn't help but look her up and down. "Normally that's a name given to someone, not chosen."

"Well, I definitely chose it for myself." She shrugged an elegant shoulder. "After all, hags are powerful and have no use for men. And since I am fabulous, I am The Hag. Capital T, capital H."

This was a woman after my own heart. "Fair enough."

The Hag eyed Tarron, who stood at my side. "Although if *you* were running around the Unseelie Court, I can't say that I would have given up men entirely."

"I'll take that as a compliment." He reached for my hand. "But as it stands, I'm taken."

The Hag's eyes moved between the two of us. "I can see that." She strolled to us, sniffing delicately at the air, as if to get a sense of our signatures. "Hmmmm. It will be difficult to conceal you."

"But not impossible?" I asked.

"Nothing is impossible for me." She gave a catlike grin and turned. "Come."

We followed her toward the cauldron, which had two chairs to the left. They hadn't been there a moment ago. I hadn't even seen her conjure them. I shot her a look, my brow raised.

"I am a woman of many talents." She turned and faced us. "Now, tell me your greatest fear."

"Uh, what?" She might as well have asked me to drop my pants. I'd probably have preferred it.

Tarron frowned. "Why?"

"Truth helps my magic."

I squinted at her. It helped her magic...or she was just curious.

"I'm serious." She went to her shelves and collected a glass jar and several clusters of dried herbs. "Take a moment to think of it."

My mind raced as she started chopping up the dried herbs.

My greatest fear.

There were so many, actually.

Losing Tarron. Losing my sister. Not defeating the false queen. Failing the Fae.

I shot a glance at Tarron.

He didn't seem even a little bit torn.

I nudged him and whispered, "You know your fear?"

"Of course. You don't?"

"I've got loads. How do I choose?"

"One has to be stronger than all the others." He nodded to The Hag. "Or she's going to be very disappointed."

If she *really* needed my greatest fear and I didn't come up with it, *I* was going to be disappointed because we'd never get the spell we needed.

The Hag worked quickly, lighting the herbs on fire and collecting the smoke in a glass jar. It swirled with gray and green light, a sickly concoction that turned my stomach.

Finally, she turned to us. "Have you thought of your greatest fear?"

I pointed to Tarron. "He can go first."

He nodded.

The Hag shot me a knowing look, but she approached Tarron and held the glass jar up. The smoke continued to swirl inside, never leaving the jar.

She held it up to his face. "Speak your greatest fear into the smoke."

Tarron took the jar, held the lip of it up to his mouth, and spoke. "Losing Mari."

I blinked, surprised. Losing him was one of my great fears, too, but I hadn't expected him to say it so easily. So confidently.

But the words rang with truth.

And the smoke seemed to know it. It brightened, turning to a brilliant blue that sparkled with life.

The Hag smiled. "It seems that you spoke true."

"Easy enough." Tarron handed the jar to me, meeting my gaze.

The smoke swirled within, taunting me.

"Um..." My mind raced. I feared so much. The idea of deciding who I was most terrified to lose—my sister or Tarron—made me want to vomit and then die. Not to mention the idea of failing all the Fae and allowing the false queen to stay in power. She'd suck the life from all of them.

So, no pressure there.

Listing them all wouldn't do it. She wanted the one great fear. The big one. And suddenly, it came to me.

"I'm not enough." I blurted it into the smoke. It flared even brighter blue, swirling with purple light and sparks.

"You spoke true as well." The Hag's eyes sparked. "I had my doubts."

"It was easy." After all, if I were strong enough, smart enough, quick enough, I could save them all. I wouldn't have to lose them, or choose which was the one I couldn't bear to be parted from.

The Hag shot me a knowing look, then took the glass jar from us. She smashed it to the ground, chanting a spell in a language I didn't recognize. Light flashed, and magic filled the air. The smoke expanded, swirling around Tarron and me as a tornado.

It filled my lungs, making me cough and my skin tingle. My muscles were next, then my bones. My entire body vibrated.

Tarron grimaced. "I presume it's working?"

"It is indeed." The Hag gestured to us. "Look at each other."

I looked at Tarron, whose form shimmered with light, turning nearly transparent.

"You'll be able to see each other, but you will be invisible to the rest of the world. Your signatures will disappear as well, until you are entirely undetectable to the protections on the queen's palace."

"What's the downside?" I asked.

"It will last a bit less than two hours. So be quick. If the spell fades while you are in enemy territory, they will immediately sense you and attack."

"Thank you."

"What do we owe you?" Tarron asked.

She looked aghast. "I do this for the Resistance."

"Then thank you."

She nodded. "Be victorious."

Strange. That was the same thing that Perisea had said to me.

Tarron turned to leave, and I went to follow, but The Hag clutched my arm, leaning close enough to whisper in my ear. "Remember who you are, or you will lose all."

I frowned at her. "I was just told that by someone else."

"Someone wise." Her eyes glinted with knowledge, then she pushed me gently. "Now go. You are running out of time."

I wanted to argue—to ask for more clarification—but she was right. We only had two hours.

I hurried after Tarron, who waited outside. The forest was quiet in this part, eerily devoid of Fae or animals.

"Let's fly," Tarron said.

I called upon my wings, launching myself into the air. Cool wind welcomed me, and we skimmed over the tree-tops, heading toward the palace.

The field that separated the forest from the city was empty at this hour. The broad stretch of grass was No Man's Land between the Resistance and the palace.

I flew faster, pushing toward answers. We soared over the field, and it prickled eerily, almost like the air were haunted. When we approached the castle walls, I called upon my shield from the ether.

Tarron looked and me, and I shrugged. "Just in case."

He nodded, and called upon his own shield.

I tensed as we neared the guard posts, praying that The Hag's potion worked as she'd promised it would. I spotted the first guard positioned near the gatehouse. My heart thundered in my ears.

He didn't look up, even though he should have caught sight of us by now.

Instead, he just leaned against the castle wall, staring idly out into space.

The other guard didn't see us, either, thank fates.

My shoulders began to relax a bit once we crossed over the city walls. Until I noticed all the people.

Were they moving slower?

I flew closer to Tarron and whispered, "Do they seem slower?"

He nodded. "A bit like robots. It's worse than before."

"The false queen's influence," I hissed. "She is sucking the life from them, growing ever stronger with each one." I couldn't imagine being that power hungry.

"She might not be queen long, at this rate."

"She'll just find new territory—new people—to use."

"Not if we have anything to say about it."

I nodded, determined. I shoved aside the fear that I couldn't take her on. It was strange, though. I'd never really suffered from insecurity. But one month with her and I was a wreck.

As we neared the castle, the feeling of dark magic grew. I wrinkled my nose against the scent of brimstone and putrid night lilies, breathing shallowly through my mouth. A sense of despair crept over me.

"You feel that?" I asked Tarron.

"I do. But ignore it. It's not real. Just her influence."

I shuddered and clung to the words. He was right—it was just the false queen's magic. But damned if it didn't feel real.

The palace rose up from the ground, huge and ornate. The towers speared the sky like daggers, and the decorative carvings seemed to swirl with menace, almost like they were moving, searching the sky for a threat.

I focused on my desire to find the well of power, calling upon my seeker sense.

Come on, let it work.

What was the point of having royal blood if it wouldn't help me do this?

Finally, it tugged. I pointed to the space behind the castle. "I think it's back there."

Tarron nodded, and we flew in a wide circle around the towers. The windows glinted with cold light, and I peered into each as we passed. In each one, I searched for the false queen. Each time, I came up empty.

Would I attack if I spotted her?

It'd be hard not to, though we really needed to cut her supply from the well of power, first.

Finally, we reached the woods behind the castle. They were creepy and dark, the trees all twisted, tiny things. Imbued with evil, unable to grow. Dark mist wafted up from the forest, and I made sure to fly above it. Thank fates we'd come by air. It would have taken too long to make it through the city on foot.

There was no sign of the well of power, though.

I squinted into the distance, catching sight of a huge field of shrubbery. Thick bushes were cropped low to the ground, calling to me.

I flew closer, spotting telltale passages through the bushes.

"A hedge maze," I said.

"Where?"

Tarron flew closer to me, and I pointed to it.

"I just see more woods."

"No way. You have to be able to see the hedge maze. It's right there."

He shook his head. "Just more trees."

"Weird." I flew closer, the sense of knowledge tugging harder at me.

The well was inside the maze. I could feel it as easily as I could feel my own heartbeat. We were nearly to it when Tarron grunted in pain.

"What is it?" I demanded, studying his face.

He blinked, his eyes widening. "I see the maze now."

I looked back toward it. We were almost over top of the first row of green bushes. "It was hidden. We must have crossed over the barrier."

"And only you could see it before."

"You have royal blood, too."

"Not Unseelie, though. It must make a difference."

I nodded, then turned my attention to the maze below. The hedges seemed to shift as I flew, changing course. I pointed. "Do you see that?"

"I do." He frowned.

I flew toward the middle, flying faster, my heart thundering.

A few moments later, I spotted it...

The well looked like any other well. Gray stones, short, rustic. The dark smoke that wafted up from it was definitely weird, but it was otherwise totally normal. Boring, even.

"I'm going for it." I flew down toward it.

"I've got your back."

I nodded, reaching into the ether for my potion bag. I plunged my hand in, and my fingers closed over the Aranthian Crystal. I pulled it out, clutching it close.

The well was about twenty yards away when the air began to prickle more fiercely. Protection charms.

I gritted my teeth and pushed myself harder, trying to get past. Soon, the prickles became a fierce sense of pain— as if I were being stabbed.

Tears stung my eyes.

"Come back," Tarron shouted.

"No!" I flew harder, trying to force myself past the barrier.

"Let me," he said. "It's too dangerous."

As if the barrier had heard him and wanted to agree, it threw up an invisible wall in front of me. I plowed into it, feeling like I was being hit in the face with a sledgehammer. It was all I could do to retain my grip on the Aranthian crystal.

I can't lose it.

I cried out, unable to help myself, and flew backward. The farther away I got, the more normal the air felt.

Tarron reached for my hand, pulling me away from the barrier. Finally, the pain stopped.

Panting, I looked at him. "Well, that didn't work."

"She'd never let anyone approach via the air."

"We'll need to approach by land." Which sucked.

"At least we know where it is, now. We'd never have made it this far on foot."

He looked at the sky. "The sun says we've only got about thirty minutes left on this potion. We need to get out of here."

Fates, that might not be enough time. We had to make it back to tell everyone where the well was. We needed backup to finish this.

I gave it one last look, then flew back toward the palace. To keep it safe, I shoved the Aranthian crystal back into my potion bag in the ether.

"Faster," Tarron urged.

I pushed my wings harder, already starting to feel the same strange chill that had come over me when The Hag's potion had first gone into effect.

We cut a closer circle around the castle, strapped for time. Again, I searched for the false queen in the windows, but didn't spot her. I could smell her, though, and it turned my stomach.

As we flew overhead, the city looked just as it had the first time, with the same tired, robotic Fae going about their daily lives. A few of them glanced toward the sky, but didn't seem to see us.

The strangest sensation came over me as we neared the guards at the wall, and I whispered to Tarron, "The potion is wearing off faster."

"I feel it."

The guards began to shift, looking around.

"They can sense our magic," Tarron murmured.

Soon, they'd be able to see us.

My heartbeat thundered, fear icing my skin. I flew as fast as I could, pushing myself to the limit. Sweat broke out, and my muscles ached.

We were right overhead when I heard one of the guards speak, confusion in his voice. "Intruders."

"I feel them but don't see them," said another.

I drew my shield from the ether, and Tarron followed suit.

We'd just flown over the wall when a guard pointed at us. "There!"

Oh, crap.

We'd been spotted.

13

I flew as fast as I could, desperate to get away from the city and the guards. We had to deliver the location of the well, or all was lost.

I looked behind me, spotting one of the guards as he threw a blast of green light at us. It hurtled toward me, and I dodged, barely avoiding a blow to the legs. A second threw a fireball that moved so fast I barely had time to get my shield up in front of me.

The flame plowed into the metal, and I tumbled backward in the air, losing control of my wings.

Tarron flew in front of me, his shield raised.

Protecting me.

The same guard hurled an even bigger fireball, and Tarron flew right toward it, taking the hit to his shield and grunting.

I righted myself in the air. "Come on!"

Tarron turned and followed me. I flew as fast as I

could, glancing behind me to see that three of the guards had launched themselves into the air and were following.

Shit. We couldn't lead them back to the Resistance camp. My heart thundered as I drew my potion bag from the ether. I dug my hand in, searching for a stunning bomb.

Tarron didn't waste time. His magic flared, and he shot a blast of air at one of the guards. It slammed into the Fae, and the man tumbled back, plowing into the ground with such force that he lay still, unconscious.

A second Unseelie threw a blast of fire at me. I chucked my potion bomb at him, then dived left, taking a hit from the fire. It grazed my thigh, making pain flare.

Frustration welled, and I screamed, "We're just trying to help you!"

A crazy queen did no one any good. Not that these guys cared.

The last Unseelie was fast, dodging Tarron's blasts of wind. When one hit him, he didn't go down.

The guy was freaking strong.

I could try to reflect his magic back on him, but it might kill him. Since we didn't know if he was truly on my mother's side or just being brainwashed, I didn't want to do it.

Unfortunately, we were already halfway toward the forest and couldn't go any farther until we lost him.

I caught Tarron's eye and mouthed, "Let's surround him."

Tarron nodded, then flew backward, getting between

the Unseelie and the city. I flew in front of him, and we cornered him, closing in from either side. He threw an icicle at me, and I darted right, barely avoiding the projectile. Icy air whistled past my face as it flew by.

I threw a stunning bomb at the same time Tarron threw a blast of air. Both slammed into the Unseelie at the same time, and he plunged to the ground. He hit hard, but not on his head, at least.

I looked back toward the castle. There were no other Fae following us, thank fates.

"Let's get the hell out of here." I turned and flew toward the forest.

Tarron joined me, and we disappeared into the safety of the trees. It was quiet and dark, the ground shaded by the canopy above. Faerie lights illuminated the way as we flew back to the camp.

When we reached the camp a few minutes later, the number of people seemed to have grown, and most were polishing weapons or mending armor.

This is it.

The realization chilled me.

The final battle was coming, and these Fae were about to risk their lives for it.

I shoved away the worry. We needed their help if we were going to win. And we were fighting *for* them, after all. Of course they'd want to be in the fight. As much as I hated the idea of thrusting innocent lives in the false queen's direction, they had the right to choose that. And truth be told, we were probably going to need their help.

I spotted Brielle near the fire. She turned to face us, watching us with a serious expression on her face.

She strode toward us. "Well?"

"We found it." I landed a few feet from her, closing my wings against my back. It was finally starting to feel truly natural to fly. "I tried to destroy it, but it's protected from aerial attack."

Tarron joined me, sticking close to my side.

She nodded. "Makes sense. Where is it?"

"In the middle of a hedge maze, past the dark forest that is on the other side of the castle."

Her lips thinned. "That will be dangerous to get to."

"I can take it."

"Good." She gestured for me to follow. "Let's eat and plan for tomorrow. Then we'll sleep."

At the mention of food, my stomach grumbled. Sleep sounded good, too.

Tarron touched my shoulder. "Go with her. I'm going to gather the rest of my troops from the Seelie Court. Four dozen. It is nearly sunset, so they could arrive tonight."

Brielle nodded. "Thank you, King Tarron."

"This is my fight as much as it is yours."

"Evil is everyone's fight." She turned and strode toward the table.

Several Fae spotted her going and hurried to join her.

I reached for Tarron and gave him a quick, hard kiss. "When this is over, I want that date."

"Which one?"

"The one we talked about in the museum."

He grinned. "It's yours."

"Good." I followed Brielle to the table.

Aeri and Declan joined us, along with the FireSouls. A Fae I didn't recognize brought over tea, and Brielle poured the cups.

I leaned forward. "I tried to deploy the Aranthian Crystal, but I couldn't get close enough to the well of power. It's blocked from the air."

Brielle cursed. "We'll need to approach from the ground, then."

"My men can act as backup," Tarron said.

"Thank you." Brielle nodded to him. "The false queen can't realize you're going for it, or she'll try to stop you."

"And she's strong enough right now that she'll manage," I said. We needed to buy enough time to destroy the well of power so she'd be weak enough to defeat.

"What we need is a distraction," Del said.

"A battle will do that," Brielle said.

"We shouldn't risk more lives than necessary. I hoped we could plan something that involves me sneaking in."

"The Hag has no more potion for you to slip into the city undetected," Brielle said. "And it wouldn't have worked from the ground anyway. You'd be too close to the people."

"We snuck in last time I was here," I said.

Brielle shook her head. "But the queen's power has grown so much that it won't work again."

"You're saying we have to fight," Aeri said.

"We have to fight to get you as far as we can into the

city," Brielle said. "All the way to the forest and the maze if we can manage it."

"That's so far. We'll lose so many lives." My heart hurt at the thought.

"Maybe not," Brielle said. "We have greater numbers. Greater power. If we're smart and plan well, I think we'll do all right."

"The queen can't know you're going toward the maze, though," Cass said. "Which means she needs to think you're a part of the battle."

"So I need to be two places at once."

She grinned. "Exactly. And I can help with that. Pick a team of three to approach the well of power. I can use my power of illusion to make me, Del, and Nix appear to be you three. We'll continue to fight with the rest in the city. The queen will believe it's you."

"I wouldn't put you at risk like that."

She smiled. "You think we can't handle it?"

Well... She had a point. Cass, Nix, and Del were insanely powerful. They could handle anything. "Are you sure?"

"Of course I'm sure." She leaned forward. "Who are you taking?"

I was strongest with Aeri and Tarron at my side.

"Me, obviously," Aeri said. "No arguments."

I looked at her. "Thank you."

Brielle leaned forward. "Now let's work out the details of our approach."

The sun set as we talked, planning the intricacies of

the attack. By the time we were done, I was starving and full dark had fallen. Faerie lights twinkled from the trees, illuminating the forest.

Somewhere, a small band of Fae had started playing music. It streamed merrily through the trees, at contrast with the somber feeling of battle on the horizon.

Brielle caught me listening and shrugged. "Some of us won't survive tomorrow. Might as well enjoy tonight."

I nodded, though the thought made my heart heavy.

Brielle stood. "Come on, the food is ready. Let's get some."

Aeri and I followed her toward the fire, collecting a bowl of hearty soup from the old Fae who manned the enormous pot. Connor helped him, moving quickly around the pot.

"Enjoy, Your Highness." Connor winked.

Yeah, that was weird. "Thank you."

He grinned.

I shared a look with Aeri as we walked away. "I'm glad I don't have to be the real queen, that's for sure."

"Best of both worlds, for you." Aeri found a seat on a log, and I joined her, pressing my shoulder against hers as we ate.

At one point, Burn appeared, taking a seat at my side. Almost immediately, one of the Fae brought the Thorn Wolf a bowl, and he gobbled it up excitedly.

Declan, who'd disappeared at some point, appeared through the crowd.

I looked at Aeri. "Love you, sis."

She raised a brow as I stood.

I nodded toward Declan, who was nearly to us. "That's my cue."

"You don't have to go."

"I want to go find my man, too."

She smiled. "I like him."

"Good, because I do, too."

Declan joined us, and I waved. "See you later."

I found Tarron at the edge of the clearing, standing with his men. There were dozens of them, all staring at him with rapt expressions. I couldn't hear what he was saying, but clearly they were impressed.

Quietly, I crept closer, wanting to hear whatever it was. I'd just gotten close enough when they began to applaud.

Dang. Missed it.

The men dispersed, and Tarron turned to face me.

I walked up to him and wrapped my arms around his neck. "It seems your troops were impressed with you."

"They're an easy crowd." He pulled me to him.

"Somehow, I doubt that." I raised a brow. "I recall the circumstances of your ascension to the throne. You had to win them over." Shadows entered his eyes, and suddenly I felt like a jerk. "I'm sorry. I didn't mean to bring up sad things."

He shook his head. "It's fine. I'll always miss my brother and regret the end of his life. That I didn't realize sooner what was happening to him." His gaze moved off to the trees and his jaw tightened. "But we're here, and I'll have vengeance for him. We'll protect anyone else from suffering his fate."

It tore me apart that my mother had been the one to pollute his brother's mind with dark magic. She'd been responsible for his death. For so many deaths.

As much as it tore me up to know that she was the cause of these things, there was still some tiny little part of me that railed against it. That didn't want to believe it.

She was my *mother.*

But Tarron—and his status as a somewhat unwilling king—were a constant reminder of what she had done.

"Have you ever considered transitioning your people over to a democracy?" I asked. "Take some of the burden off you? Let them rule themselves?"

He smiled. "I like that idea."

"I'm clever."

"When this is over, that can be our next goal."

I pressed a kiss to his lips. "I like having goals with you. Especially ones that don't involve fighting to stay alive."

"One might say that's the biggest goal of all."

"Sure, and I'd agree. But I'm looking forward to a life that I can enjoy rather than just survive."

"Can't blame you." He squeezed me to him. "We'll try to convert the Seelie Court to a democracy."

"Really?"

"Really. Besides being the right thing to do, it will give us more time for each other."

He had a point. Between me being a demon slayer, Blood Sorceress, and partial queen, I was going to be busy.

As full-time king, he wouldn't be able to leave his kingdom much. Especially since he'd been gone so much while we hunted the false queen.

"First, we need to defeat the false queen," I said. "Then we'll deal with that."

If we could defeat the false queen. And that was a big if.

After our talk, Tarron and I found Brielle, who led us to an empty bird's nest house. It sat about fifty feet up, nestled in the branches of a huge tree.

She pointed to it. "You can have that one."

"Thank you." I smiled at her. "We'll see you at dawn."

She nodded, her gaze serious. Brielle hadn't cracked a smile yet, and I couldn't blame her. Not with what waited on the horizon for us. Silently, she disappeared back into the forest.

"Let's go." I called upon my wings and flew up to the strange little house made of thin reeds that had been woven together. The door swung open easily, revealing a beautiful room that looked nothing like the outside.

It was built entirely of pale wood decorated with intricate carvings, and the enormous bed was covered in blue silk.

Tarron joined me, his gaze going straight to the bed. "Fit for a queen."

"Oh?" I smiled and turned to him.

Before I could say anything, his strong hands closed around my waist, and he pulled me to him. I gasped, reaching up to grab his shoulders. His mouth crashed down on mine, and I moaned, pressing myself closer to him.

The world disappeared as he kissed me, all of my fears disappearing as the only thing I could focus on became him. He pulled me to him so I could feel every inch of his hard body against mine.

It could be our last night together. The thought tore at my heart, but I forced it away. Gasping, I grappled with his shirt, tearing it off. My shirt got the same treatment, buttons popping as he dragged it from me.

Frantic, I ran my hands over his chest, reveling in the strength of his muscles.

"You're so beautiful." Heat burned in his eyes as his gaze swept over me.

I kissed his neck, determined to taste every inch of him.

He groaned and dropped his head back, clutching me to him. His scent filled me, making my mind grow cloudy with lust.

"I'll never want anything more than I want you," he rasped.

The truth was, I couldn't agree more.

The dream hit me, hard and fast.

I stood in the middle of an empty, dark space.

All alone.

Just me, in my human form.

No Fae wings, no nothing.

The false queen surged toward me, her black wings carrying her gracefully on the air. Her voice was cold as she hissed, "You are mine now, daughter."

I cried out and stumbled backward, clumsily trying to go for my weapons. But no matter how hard I tried, I couldn't access the ether to get them.

She reached me, going for my throat. Her hands closed around my neck, cutting off the air. I struggled, trying to break her grip, but I was too weak.

"You're nothing," she hissed.

I'm not!

I couldn't even say the words. My dream self didn't even try. I attempted to call on my wings, but it was no good. I couldn't even cut my wrist with my nails to try to make new magic.

One last try.

And I couldn't manage it.

I was helpless.

Every weapon I'd ever had abandoned me.

And now she was here.

And I was dying.

14

I woke on a scream, the dark light of morning a cocoon around me.

"Mari!" Tarron lunged for me and wrapped me in his arms.

Gasping, I tried to get ahold of myself. Tears streaked down my cheeks, and I gripped him close.

"What was it?" he asked. "A dream?"

The last thing I remembered was dying, but I didn't tell him that. I sucked in a ragged breath and pulled away. "I don't want to think about it."

He drew back, his gaze concerned. "You can tell me."

"I don't even want to tell myself." I couldn't bear to think of it. A therapist would probably tell me I needed to explore it for hidden messages—only a dummy would think that dream hadn't been loaded with my worst fears —but I just couldn't face it.

I climbed out of the bed, trying to still my shaking. "Let's go."

"You're afraid." Tarron frowned. "You're never afraid."

I gave a slightly bitter laugh. "Of course I'm afraid. Who wouldn't be?"

"Only an idiot, I suppose. But this is different."

I frowned at him, hating that he was right. I'd been afraid many times in my life—I wasn't a moron. I'd faced down some truly deadly shit, so of course I'd faced fear.

But this...

This was awful.

Because I was afraid of myself. Afraid of my ability—or lack of ability—to get the job done when everything was on the line.

I sucked in a deep breath and shoved the thought away. I just had to do it. There was no other choice. Dwelling on it wouldn't help.

I reached for Tarron and grabbed his hand, pulling him up from the bed. "Come on. Let's go."

He stood, his concerned gaze heavy on my face. I couldn't bear it. That kind of concern burned like acid. I wanted to be the confident Mordaca I'd once been, and when he looked at me like that, it was all too clear that I *wasn't*.

I pressed a hard kiss to his lips, both so I wouldn't have to see his face and because I wanted to, then I spun and began to dress.

Fear didn't mean I had to lie down and cry.

Tarron's magic flared, and he handed me a freshly conjured shirt to replace the one he'd ripped last night.

"Thanks." I shot him a smile, and though it wasn't one of my best, it seemed to make him feel a bit better. Or he'd figured out that I didn't like the concern. I appreciated it, but I didn't like it.

Soon, we were dressed.

I strode to the door. I was about to pull the door open when he gripped my arm and pulled me to him.

Reluctantly, I met his gaze.

"You may not believe in yourself," he said. "But I believe in you."

My throat tightened unbearably, and all I could do was nod, my lips pressed tight together. I turned away, sucking in a deep breath as I pushed the door open.

Crowds of fighters had already gathered in the clearing. I could see them through the trees—hundreds of them, prepared for battle. My gaze went to my sister immediately, somehow able to find her without trouble. I could do that with Tarron, too, I realized.

I shot Tarron a look over my shoulder. "I love you."

I turned back to the crowd and flew to the ground. They turned to look at me, and I straightened my shoulders. Tarron joined me, and I caught the look he gave me.

Say something.

I drew in a deep breath, shoving the fear down deep. They didn't need to see that. Slowly, I moved my gaze over the crowd, then spoke so my voice rang out, heavy with the gravity of the situation. "We fight for *freedom*. Together.

Your home has been invaded from the inside by a terrible dictator. But we will defeat her. Together. And when we win, *you* will have control of your own destiny."

That was it.

I could say more words, but those were the important ones.

Fortunately, everyone agreed. Cheers rang out, and the Fae raised their weapons, shaking them to the sky.

I shivered and shared a look with Aeri.

This was *really* never where I'd expected to be. Leading a crowd of hundreds into battle. Not my scene.

Life threw curveballs at you sometimes.

"I'm going to speak to my troops briefly," Tarron said.

I pressed a kiss to his cheek, then launched myself into the air and flew to Brielle, who waited at the back of the crowd, closest to the forest exit. I landed in front of her.

Finally, she cracked the smallest smile. "Good job."

"Thanks. Not really my normal."

"This is no one's normal."

"It is yours." I looked back at the camp. "You've been keeping things going here. You should lead us into battle."

She nodded, her jaw firm, then turned. She raised her spear and then started into the forest. I followed her. Aeri joined me, along with Tarron and Declan. The FireSouls caught up, and we moved swiftly through the woods.

Every now and then, I glanced back to see the fighters behind us. Hundreds of them, steely-eyed and determined.

We broke through the forest as the sun was rising. It shed a golden glow over the field, somehow managing to cast the city in shadow. Or perhaps that was the false queen's influence.

We made it across the field without issue.

We were three quarters of the way across when Aeri spoke at my side. "It's weird. None of the guards are coming to greet us."

"They don't want to leave the safety of the fortress," I said.

"Not safe for long."

"No. Not for long." Our goal would not be to kill—just in case those we fought were under the influence of the dark queen. Brielle had passed the word around last night, and since most of these Unseelie Fae had left loved ones behind in the city, they were quick to agree.

As we neared the city walls, shouts sounded from behind it. Fae guards gathered at the top of the walls, pointing toward us.

I could hear the shock in their voices, and it surprised me. "I'd have thought they'd expect this."

"Brainwashing is powerful," Brielle said. "They may not even realize there is a Resistance."

Spears began to fly, blasts of magic following. Our core guard rushed to the front, holding up massive shields in front of the troops. Weapons and blasts of magic exploded against the shields, throwing some of the guards back. Others replaced them.

Tarron launched himself into the air, a shield covering his body as he threw out his hand. His magic surged, and an enormous gust of wind exploded from his palm. It drove the flying weapons and spells back at the Unseelie who had fired them.

They shouted and dived, taking cover behind the walls. The blasts of magic—all colors of the rainbow—exploded against the castle walls. Huge holes appeared, and sections of rock tumbled to the ground.

Tarron turned back to his troops and shouted, "Earth powers!"

He waved his arm, and his magic swelled on the air. Other Seelie joined him, stepping forward, their magic swelling. There had to be at least two dozen of them, all with the power of manipulating the earth. They joined their king, and a massive wave of magic exploded from them, rushing toward the city wall.

The ground beneath the wall began to shake, an enormous crevasse opening up right underneath.

The stone gatehouse was the first to fall, tumbling into the giant pit. A dozen Unseelie guards launched themselves off the top of the gatehouse, flying to the safety of the air.

Connor raced forward, shouting, "Stunners, attack!"

His troop of Fae—all of whom had been chosen for their excellent aim—followed him to the front, stopping right behind the line of shields. The guards shifted to get lower, giving the stunners room to throw. They hurled potion bombs into the air, aiming for the Unseelie who flew above the collapsing wall.

Glass potion bombs exploded against the Unseelies' chests, and they swayed, flying clumsily into the city, their wings faltering as the stunning bombs took effect. Connor had modified them so the Fae wouldn't drop on the spot. Falling could be deadly, even for one with wings.

Within minutes, a huge section of castle wall had fallen into the earth, and dozens of Unseelie guards had been taken out by Connor's stunning potions.

"Go!" Brielle shouted. She ran forward, and the troops followed.

Time to storm the castle.

Tarron flew toward the city, moving his arm in an arc. The crevasse began to close up, forming a bridge for the land bound to walk across. Though most of our troops were Fae and could fly, our plan revolved around sticking together on the ground.

We reached the edge of the city and raced over the uneven ground. Ahead of us, a huge avenue stretched into the city, all the way up to the palace steps.

Like a red carpet that would be made crimson by blood. I shook away the terrible thought. We'd avoid that fate. I'd see to it.

Unseelie guards and citizens alike rushed toward the avenue, appearing on sidewalks and at the front of their homes.

"Declan, lightning!" Brielle shouted.

Declan launched himself into the air, his feathered angel wings carrying him high. He raised his hands, and his magic surged. Lightning struck, hundreds of bolts shooting straight into the ground on either side of the avenue.

Declan had amazing control, because not a single bolt hit a Fae—Seelie or Unseelie. They did cut them off from the avenue, however, giving us mostly unobstructed access to the palace beyond.

"Forward!" Brielle shouted.

Our side surged ahead, racing down the massive street. Some of the Unseelie had been trapped with us in the street, but Connor and his troops took care of them with potion bombs. Nix followed behind, conjuring protective cages over their unconscious bodies—we didn't need anyone getting trampled.

No doubt some of these Unseelie fought with the false queen because they wanted to. There were a few bad apples in every group. But we'd sort that out after the battle.

We were halfway down the avenue when Aeri muttered, "Too easy."

"The false queen will be here soon," Brielle said. "You won't be saying that then."

As if she'd heard us, a scream rent the air. Though I couldn't see her anywhere, it was so loud that my ears rang. The noise brought with it a massive wind that blasted Declan's lightning away. Unseelie surged into the street, their weapons raised.

Shit.

We'd planned for this—not how it would happen, but what could happen. Still, it was terrifying. This wasn't an enemy we could just kill.

"Barriers!" Brielle shouted.

Nix raced forward, her dark hair flying behind her and her magic surging. She raised her hands, and barriers appeared on the side of the street. Tarron's magic joined hers, and the fences grew up in an arc over the street.

The Unseelie launched themselves into the air, shooting magic down into the street. I raised my shield, covering my head from an aerial attack. Next to me, Aeri and Brielle did the same.

Connor and his crew threw potion bombs up into the air, stunning some of the attacking Unseelie. They lost control and fell, collapsing onto the tunnel of fencing that protected us.

Nix turned and caught Brielle's eye. "I can't hold it much longer!"

A few moments later, the Unseelie began to break through the barrier. We were nearly to the castle, and the fight was about to begin in earnest.

Dozens of Unseelie landed on the street with us, raising their weapons and attacking. Del adopted her phantom form and raced into the crowd. They swung their blades at her, but the silver passed right through. She went corporeal long enough to grab their weapons and toss them to the Seelie who flew overhead.

Ahead of me, golden magic swirled around Cass. She transformed into her griffon form alongside Aiden, her mate. The two of them launched themselves skyward, their powerful wings beating the air.

They swooped through the sky, grabbing Unseelie in their claws and carrying them off, away from the battle.

All around, as the Unseelie converged upon us, our troops were forced into battle. It was riskier for our side, because, unlike those we fought, we weren't out for blood.

We did our best to wound but not kill as we fought our way toward the palace. I just needed to reach the forest beyond...

Another shriek rent the air, this one coming from much closer.

"She's getting pissed," Aeri said.

Lightning struck in the distance, thunder booming.

Shit.

The smaller griffon landed at my side. Golden light swirled, and Cass appeared. She dragged me into a little alley. An Unseelie tried to follow us, and she punched him hard in the face, knocking him unconscious. She dragged him to the stoop of an indented doorway so he wouldn't be trampled.

In the alley, she turned to me. "Time for you to go."

"Are you sure?" My gaze flicked to the lightning that continued to strike. "She's more deadly than ever."

Cass grinned. "So am I." She poked me. "Now get ready."

Her magic flared again, and an illusion settled over her. Black hair replaced her red, and she grew several inches. Black clothes replaced her denim and brown leather, and she grinned, red lips stretching wide.

It was like looking in a mirror.

"Fates, that's crazy." I fumbled in my pocket for the potion that would make me look like a non-descript

Unseelie. Brielle had given it to me last night. Quickly, I chugged it.

The taste of sour vinegar exploded on my tongue, and I felt my skin grow cold as the illusion overtook me.

I spoke into my comms charm. "Aeri, get in here. Little alley to the right."

Cass nodded. "It worked. You look different. Boring. But different enough."

I pointed at her. "And you look fabulous."

Aeri joined us, pinching me to make sure I was real.

"It's me."

Del appeared at her side, still incorporeal. Her blue form gleamed, semi-transparent—until Cass's magic extended to her. Then she became Aeri, shifting to become blonde and willowy.

Next to me, Aeri drank her own potion, becoming a person I didn't recognize. Besides the eyes. Those stayed normal, and I was grateful.

Nix raced up, dark hair flying. Her T-shirt was speckled with blood—a good bit of it hers, from the look of the wound on her shoulder—and it partially concealed the cartoon cat who appeared to be riding on a rainbow Pop-Tart.

"Dibs on Tarron!" she shouted.

Cass grinned, which was weird because she looked like me when she did it. "Good, because that's all that's left."

A moment later, Tarron appeared. He reached into his pocket, withdrawing a little vial. As Nix transformed into him, he adopted the looks of another person entirely. A boring one, but at least I could recognize him in the eyes.

Del pulled her comms charm off her neck and handed me the necklace. "Here. It's connected to Nix and Cass. Once you get the Aranthian crystal into the well, we'll contact you when the people are no longer under her influence."

"Now go." Cass gave me a little shove. "Seriously, don't worry about us."

"I can't stop that, but I'll go." I caught her eye. "And thank you. From the bottom of my heart."

"We'll hold her off," Cass said.

I prayed they could last until I'd cut off her source at the well of power. Only then would we really have a chance at beating her.

As if she could read my thoughts, Cass said, "Don't worry. We can take it."

The three of them raced out into the fight, becoming bait.

Aeri, Tarron, and I sprinted out behind them.

The battle had turned into chaos, but we'd nearly reached the palace. The three of us raced through the crowd, dodging the fight as we headed to the dark forest and the maze beyond.

In the sky, the false queen burst out of the glass windows in the highest tower, a shriek of rage accompanying her. Her black lace gown glittered as if it were made of diamonds, and I hated that she looked better with every ounce of power that she gained.

Her black and white hair was swept into an updo that was threaded through with massive spikes. Her black wings were bigger than ever, carrying her down toward the crowd.

"Hurry!" Aeri said.

I turned my attention away from the false queen and sprinted past the palace. The dark forest was right ahead of us, the twisted trees crouching low to the ground.

My lungs burned as we ran, leaving behind the sounds of battle as the shadows enveloped us. Guilt streaked through me at the idea of my friends left behind to fight in my place, but this was the only way to beat her.

Even the faerie lights in this forest were dim, and the darkness seemed to creep into my very soul. The trees began to shudder.

"Something is coming," Tarron said.

Roots popped out of the ground around us, reaching for our ankles. I kicked one away, then called on my sword, swiping out to slice them off.

Green acid shot out of the broken root, splashing onto my skin. It burned fiercely.

"Don't cut them!" I cried.

"I've got it." Tarron's magic swelled, and it forced the roots back.

They shuddered and fought, but eventually curled back on themselves.

"Nice work," Aeri said.

We sprinted past them, jumping over the few that

managed to break past Tarron's control. They were sluggish, though, and easy to avoid.

When we spilled out of the forest, the hedge walls that created the maze rose up high in front of us. Dark magic rolled out from the maze, and smoke wafted from the tops of the bushes. The place radiated deadly threat.

"Holy fates." Worry echoed in Aeri's voice. "We're going in *there*?"

"Yep."

15

I SUCKED IN A DEEP BREATH AND APPROACHED THE MAZE. Dark magic emanated from it, reeking of the false queen's signature.

I grimaced. "Anyone see an entrance?"

Tarron launched himself into the air and did a quick flyover. He returned a moment later. "There is no entrance."

"Damn it, of course." Just our luck.

Tarron turned to the maze, his magic flaring. Nothing happened. He strode closer and tried again. Still nothing.

He glanced back at us. "My power can't manipulate it."

"The plants are imbued with the false queen's dark magic." I drew my sword from the ether and approached.

Determination filled me as I swung my blade, slicing through the first layer of branches. They began to grow back, but I moved quicker, swinging as fast as I could, hacking away at the greenery. It reeked like brimstone and putrid night lilies, and I held my breath.

Aeri and Tarron joined me, attacking with their own blades. We cut our way through to the interior of the maze, scrambling over the sharp hedges and arriving in a long corridor.

Immediately, the hedge wall grew back into place behind us.

"Which way?" Aeri asked.

I closed my eyes and drew in a deep breath, then coughed on the stench. Aeri patted me on the back.

"Okay, apparently breathing is not an option," I said.

"As if this weren't hard enough." Aeri's eyes—the only part of her that looked like her—sparkled.

I called upon my seeker sense, trying to focus on my connection with the false queen. It was awful, though. This place smelled like her, felt like her. And made me want to be *nothing* like her.

I'd wanted magic like hers so I could defeat her.

But now that I was faced with it...

It seemed like a terrible idea.

So I focused on my skill—my seeker sense. I'd created this magic on my own, with my Dragon Blood. *That's* what I would use to defeat her.

It felt like a revelation, though it shouldn't have.

But my seeker sense worked, pulling me to the left. "This way."

I sprinted forward, and Tarron and Aeri followed. We raced through the maze, leaping over branches that struck out to attack. Sharp thorns made contact with my skin, drawing blood. The wounds burned like acid.

Tarron conjured three chain mail coats and handed them to us. I struggled into mine while running. Once I was wearing it, the thorny vines lodged in the divots between the chain mail—but they didn't cut.

We reached a crossroads, and my seeker sense pulled me right.

The deeper we got, the worse the magic felt.

"Do you feel that?" Aeri asked.

I shuddered, nodding. Dark smoke was now rolling along the ground, freezing my feet and climbing up my legs. Horrible images started to flash in my mind.

Every minute of my time with Aunt rolled through my head. All of the hungry hours, the cold hours, the scared hours. Fearing that I would lose Aeri. That I would lose myself.

Being forced to make magic that scared me. Magic that I didn't want.

I shuddered and reached for Aeri and Tarron's hands. They gripped me tight, and we ran. Just touching them made some of the cold memories fade.

"That helps," Aeri said.

"Aye." Tarron's voice was rough with pain.

The memories continued to pull on me, however, threatening to take me to my knees.

I focused on the hedge wall ahead of me, running toward it with one goal—survive to deploy the Aranthian crystal. It took forever. Hours, days, years. I was lost in the terrible memories, tears pouring down my face as I ran.

I couldn't take it.

I couldn't.

I stumbled, nearly going to my knees, but Tarron and Aeri pulled me onward.

When they stumbled, I pulled on them.

Together, finally, we reached the end of the passage.

But the path didn't turn left or right as I'd hoped. It stopped.

The black mist collected more heavily, stabbing into my mind with every awful thing that I could imagine for the future. Instead of facing my dark past, I was overcome with visions of failure. Visions of losing everyone I loved. Visions of failing the Fae.

Screw this.

I drew in a ragged breath and raised my sword, hacking at the hedge. It towered overhead, and this time, my blade wasn't able to cut into it at all. It clanged into the branches and leaves, not leaving a single dent.

"My blade isn't working either," Tarron growled.

"Same," Aeri hissed in frustration.

"Over. We have to go over." Nothing was going to stop me now.

I stashed my blade in the ether and grabbed the branches in front of me. They cut deep, making pain surge. I yanked my hands back and shook them. "Shit. The branches are sharp."

I called upon my wings, but they didn't come. Damn it,

I couldn't fly while in the maze. Some kind of magic made it impossible—no doubt to force us to face the deadly hedges.

Tarron's magic flared, and he handed me a pair of metal gloves.

"At least that magic works," I said.

"I think my magic is fading, though," he said. "The closer we get to the well, the weaker it gets."

The gloves were uncomfortable and awkward when I yanked them on, but when I gripped the branches, they didn't cut me.

I scrambled up the side of the hedge wall, trying to keep my leather-clad legs away from the sharper bits. Pain cut through my knees, but I ignored it and hauled myself over. Tarron and Aeri followed, and we threw ourselves over the top at the same time.

I sailed to the ground and landed in a crouch, looking up into the face of a huge, fanged monster.

Shit!

I lunged to the right, kicking out with my heel. My boot smashed into the face of the beast, and it lunged backward, shaking its head.

"Watch out! Monsters!" I called my shield from the ether. I crouched behind it and took stock of the situation as quickly as I could.

We were in the center of the maze, thank fates. It was large, about thirty yards in diameter. In the middle sat the stone well, surrounded by four massive monsters.

Dark magic wafted around them, reeking of the false

queen's signature scent. They were built like enormous boars, with huge horns and fang-filled mouths. Putrid green breath wafted from their lips, and their eyes glowed with flames.

"We'll cover you," Tarron said. "Get to the well."

The monsters converged on us, stalking closer. They stared hard at us, their eyes dead. Their chests didn't rise with their breaths. They were simply manifestations of the false queen's magic—not living and breathing creatures. The green smoke that emitted from their mouths was more weapon than breathing.

Tarron's magic flared briefly, then flickered out, dying a quick death. His jaw hardened. "No magic. Weapons only."

I tried anyway, attempting to call on my wings. They stayed dormant.

This damned maze.

The monsters prowled closer. I shook off the metal gloves and heavy chain mail coat. I'd need speed, and mail wouldn't protect me from those massive fangs or claws.

I called on my sword, having to push harder with my magic to make it possible. The well continued to make it difficult, but finally, I managed. I sprinted forward, racing around to the side of one. Tarron and Aeri joined me, running ahead to get between me and the monsters. They took the blows as I hurtled toward the well.

One of the beasts got between me and my target. The green smoke wafted from its mouth, and I held my breath.

It roared and charged.

I didn't slow. I raised my blade and sprinted toward the

beast. Rage and fear propelled me. This wasn't what I'd wanted for my life—far from it. I faced down demons on the daily because *I* wanted to.

This time, I had no choice in.

But it was also the most important battle I would face.

And this ugly beast stood between me and my goal. I was going through it. The creature was so tall that it towered over me. Instead of swinging my blade to attack, I slid under the legs, stabbing my blade up to the creature's middle.

The steel plunged deep, and disgusting dark smoke billowed out. I held my breath, jerking my blade hard as the creature thrashed to get away.

I yanked the blade free and scrambled out from under it, whirling to kick it in the side. When my boot collided with its ribs, the creature exploded in a poof of black dust and disappeared.

To my left and right, Tarron and Aeri battled the other three monsters, keeping them off my back.

"Go!" Aeri shouted. "Hurry!"

I sprinted for the well, drawing my potion bag from the ether as I ran. Immediately, my hand found the Aranthian crystal. The well loomed in front of me, so close I could smell the foul water at the bottom.

In the distance, the false queen shrieked. The rage was so evident, so obvious...

She was onto us.

And she was coming.

I called upon my amplification magic, feeding it into

the crystal, trying to make the magic stronger. The power in this well was immense, and I needed to freeze it solid if we were to have any hope. In my palm, the crystal pulsed with power.

I slammed into the well, leaning over the top edge and chucking the crystal into the depths. As the sparkling gem disappeared, the false queen's rage grew nearer and nearer. I called upon more of my amplification magic, trying to force it to the crystal.

"Did you do it?" Aeri shouted.

I spun around, spotting her destroy the last of the beasts with Tarron's help.

Behind me, the magic that pulsed from the well...died.

I spun around.

There was no more black smoke coming from it.

Del's charm sparked with magic, vibrating against my neck. Cass's voice echoed out. "It worked! The Fae are no longer under her spell." Her tone turned serious. "And it looks like the false queen is headed your way."

I swallowed hard, fear icing my veins.

"Hold out," Cass said. "We're following her. We're coming."

I looked to the sky, spotting the ominous figure of the false queen flying against a lightning-riddled sky. The electric bolts seemed to shoot from her. She hurtled toward us, so fast that it was almost impossible to follow her with my eyes.

I darted behind the well, but she was too quick. She

was upon us in moments, thrusting out her hand and heaving a blast of golden magic at me.

My heart rocketed into my throat.

This was what had hit Tarron!

It slammed into the well, breaking the rock wall and causing it to tumble into the pit. I scrambled away, and she fired another shot. I used all my strength to dive aside, but it hit me in the legs, sending me rolling across the grass. Pain exploded through my body, making my vision go dark.

Screaming started in my head—*my* screaming. I could feel her magic trying to overpower me, but I fought it. I poured everything I had into fighting the desperate desire not to fall victim to her power.

Agony tore through my skull as I dragged my eyes open. I spotted Aeri right as she got hit by the same golden light. Then Tarron.

They lay completely still.

No!

They couldn't be dead. They couldn't.

Weakly, I tried to drag myself away from the well, but the false queen's magic was too strong inside me. It compelled my limbs to stay still and limp. My mind buzzed with her power as her magic attempted to take over my thoughts. Terror followed quick on its heels.

Was this what Tarron had fought against this whole time?

I'd been right to fear it.

A dozen yards away, Aeri tried to crawl to me. She was

weak, but had gained consciousness. Thank fates she was so strong, or she'd have fallen to the false queen's power. Behind her, Tarron was stirring, beginning to sit up.

The bitch herself landed between us, shooting a glance between Aeri and me. She flung out her hand and hit Aeri with another blast.

My sister collapsed, unconscious.

The queen turned toward Tarron, and delivered a second blow.

"No!" I screamed. The sound was hoarse, weak, and the false queen laughed.

"You cannot fight me!" She strode toward me, victory glowing on her face.

"We froze the well of power."

A scowl flashed across her face. "True. But I am still here, am I not?"

"Not as strong as you were." I dragged myself upright, managing to only get as far as propping myself on my elbows. If she were as strong as she'd been, I'd be totally under her spell like Tarron had been. Instead, we'd bought ourselves a bit of time.

Except I was too weak to do anything with it.

It was all my nightmares come true.

She crouched next to me, her eyes gleaming with malice. "You think you've won, but you've put yourself right where I want you."

What were my friends doing outside the forest?

Were they dead?

Tears smarted my eyes at the idea, and I forced them

back. Now was *not* the time for weakness. I struggled to drag myself away from her, and she laughed.

"You are too weak." An evil smile crossed her face. "Just as I always suspected. Just like I said. I cannot believe that I invited you to join me."

"Never." I spit at her.

She slapped me, and pain flared, igniting my rage.

"No," she said. "You are better used for my purposes."

She grabbed my arm and sliced my wrist with her sharp fingernail. Black blood welled, and she gave a satisfied smirk. "The tainted one."

"Tainted by you." Even as I said it, I hated the words.

It wasn't true.

I wasn't tainted.

The Unseelie weren't evil.

She was evil.

And I didn't want to be anything like her. Not even to have her strength. I could see now how wrong I'd been to seek that. It really did lead to the darkness.

I tried to yank my wrist back, but she gripped it tight, tilting it over to pour the blood into a little glass vial she procured from the pocket of her dress.

The blood dripped slowly into the vial, and she huffed a frustrated sound. "Too slow."

She stood and began dragging me toward the well. "I'll just throw you in. It requires your blood, so why not give it all of you?"

Dread opened a hole in my stomach. She was going to *throw me in?*

My wings didn't work within the maze, and she was going to throw me into that horrible dark well?

"Don't worry," she said. "You won't be alone. Your sister will be with you. I need both of your blood to become all-powerful."

"No!" I thrashed, trying to break her grip.

She tightened it and dragged me faster. I called upon my sword, yanking it from the ether and slicing out for her. She grabbed the blade with her hand, blood running from between her fingers, and yanked it away with incredible strength.

"Thank you, I needed this." She tossed it into the air and caught the hilt, then slashed toward me.

The tip of the sword sliced across my chest. Pain flared and blood welled. She struck out again, slicing my shoulder.

I screamed and tried to jerk away, but she kept going.

"We need to make sure the well gets plenty of your blood," she said. "And your sister's. *Then* I will be all-powerful, and I shall never be caged again."

"You're a monster," I hissed.

"About to become a better one, because of you. How clever I was to have a Dragon Blood for a daughter."

Bile rose in my throat at the thought. I called upon my bag of potion bombs. No way I'd go down without a fight. But I was weak—slow from blood loss.

By the time I got the bag, we were to the edge of the well. She said nothing as she shoved me in. Just kicked me over the edge as if I were garbage.

I screamed as I fell into the darkness and then crashed to the rocks below. Pain sang through every inch of me as misery exploded.

This was everything that I'd feared.

And it was coming true.

Worse, she was about to do to Aeri what she'd done to me.

A howl of despair tore from my throat. I could barely move, I was so broken and bloody. Trapped, in a pit.

By my own mother.

How had I ever wanted to have her power? Even just to fight her?

Anything associated with her was evil.

I couldn't let her do this to Aeri. The mere thought made me want to die.

Remember who you are.

Perisea's words echoed in my mind.

What had she meant by that? I *knew* who I was. Mordaca, half Unseelie, half Dragon Blood. Mostly dead, bleeding out on the stones at the bottom of a putrid well.

The blood that coated me was sticky, turning cold as my life drained away.

Dragon Blood.

Remember who you are.

Wait...

Had I been going about this all wrong?

I'd been so obsessed with the idea of fighting fire with fire that I'd tried to become like the false queen.

What I'd really needed was to become more like myself.

Her strength had made me doubt myself. But that was all wrong. I was a Dragon Blood, and I had something she didn't. I couldn't fight the most powerful Fae with Fae talents.

My blood was the reason that Aunt had tortured me my entire childhood, but it could save me now. In truth, I'd shyed away from making huge magic my entire life.

Now I had to create the biggest magic there was....the most quintessential type of Dragon Blood magic.

I had to fight her as a dragon.

I had to use what made me special, and *that* was it. A dragon was also the only thing powerful enough to maybe defeat her.

I might not even be capable, but I had to try.

She'd already done half the work for me, at least. Most of my blood was gone already, seeping into the well to feed her own power. She hadn't realized what a weapon she'd given me. I was too broken to even move, pain and darkness blinding me, but I didn't *need* to move.

Instead, I called upon my magic, forcing it out with my draining blood. I was already lightheaded, so the effort was nearly too much for me. I gasped in a breath, reaching for strength.

Burn appeared next to me, whimpering low in his throat. He pressed his thorny side against mine, lending me his strength.

"Thanks, buddy." The words were garbled as they left my throat, but his strength kept me going.

As I forced my magic out of me, I focused on him, on thoughts of Aeri and Tarron and all the Fae.

I can do this. For them. For me.

I imagined becoming a dragon, as big and strong as Perisea. Stronger than the false queen. Strong enough to defeat her.

This was such an insane power—such an amazing power—that I'd never imagined adopting it for myself. I didn't even know if it was possible.

But I had to try.

Weakness tugged at my limbs, making my head spin even more. Numbness overtook me.

Fear followed.

What if I really wasn't enough? What if I couldn't do this?

No.

I can.

Burn stayed by my side as the last of my blood, the last of my magic, flowed onto the rocks. My heartbeat fluttered weakly in my ears, but my determination roared strong.

I am enough.

16

THE MAGIC IN THE AIR SPARKED, CHANGING. IT RUSHED BACK into me, more powerful than ever. I gasped, jerking upright. Strength and energy flowed through me, making my head spin and my muscles tear.

Pain followed, but it brought with it a sense of power. I surged upright, and Burn lunged back. He disappeared, as if sensing that change was coming.

My muscles expanded, my bones lengthened. Pain and power flowed through me, and wings burst from my back. I shot toward the sky, growing as I flew.

I hurtled toward the light, desperate to reach Aeri in time. As I neared the surface, I continued to grow. My wings scraped the side of the well, and I burst through to the surface with a triumphant shriek.

It felt as if the sun gave me strength, and I grew, my body becoming stronger and more powerful. My vision sharpened as well.

I searched the ground, finding the false queen dragging Aeri toward the well. Aeri had transformed back to her normal self, perhaps because of her wounds. Several horrifying cuts marred her body, and I shrieked my rage. Several yards away, Tarron was dragging himself to his feet. He, too, looked like himself again.

I dove down through the sky, hurtling toward the false queen.

She looked up, shock flashing across her face. I grabbed her with my talons, which I only now noticed were a sparkling black. I gripped her around the waist with long talons and darted toward the sky, getting her as far away from Aeri as possible.

Tarron stumbled toward Aeri, and I knew he'd use his healing gift to fix her.

The false queen shrieked, sending a blast of powerful magic exploding through me. My talons slackened, and I dropped her.

She plunged toward the ground, her wings flaring behind her back as she fell.

In the distance, I spotted our army charging through the dark forest. It was Seelie and Unseelie alike, the false queen's dark curse having been broken. On the ground, Tarron knelt over Aeri, feeding his healing light into her. Declan hurtled toward them, his black wings carrying him fast toward his love.

I turned my attention toward the false queen, who had righted herself and was now charging me, her hand outstretched to throw some of her horrible golden magic at me. It shot from her palm, fast and terrifying.

I dodged, my wings carrying me swiftly out of the way.

A sense of triumph surged through me.

I *was* strong enough. I'd just had to embrace what made me *me*.

I shot toward her, gathering my flames inside my chest. When I was close enough to see the whites of her eyes, I blasted her. The flame that shot from my mouth was brilliant green. It enveloped her. A shriek rent the air.

When the flame faded, she was still flying. Not burned —not in the traditional sense. But her magic was dampened.

My flame could destroy her power!

It was connected to the gift that I'd gotten from the Dragon Bloods—the same one that had driven her curse from Tarron's soul. I could feel the link inside me.

She flung out her hand, throwing another blast of golden magic at me. It was even slower this time, and I darted to the side, avoiding it easily. I hit her again, blasting her with the green flame.

She howled, trying to fly away, but I was too quick.

When the green flame faded, her magic gleamed even dimmer around her.

It was the strangest sort of fire I'd ever seen. Like soul fire.

On the ground below, the hordes of Unseelie Fae had broken through the false queen's maze. They'd trampled the bushes in their haste, destroying the magic that encapsulated this place and had made Fae flying impossible.

Dozens of them launched themselves into the air, flying toward me and the false queen. Screams of rage echoed from the group, and it was clear what they wanted...

Vengeance on the queen who had done so much wrong.

They should have it.

I called upon my soul fire one last time, blasting her with it. I drove her into their waiting hands, killing my flame as she neared them.

They grabbed her, and she shrieked. Her magic was neutralized now, my green flame having done its work. She disappeared inside the horde of angry Fae, and I felt it when she died. It was like a little pop on the air, and a sense of freedom.

I spun, flying back toward Aeri and Tarron. I landed hard, still unused to my new form. I looked down briefly, spotting huge black scaled feet and ebony claws. To the left and right were two enormous black and green wings. They sparkled like gems in the light.

I turned my attention toward Aeri. Her eyes were opening, and the wounds had closed. Declan had taken over the healing for Tarron, and he didn't look nearly so afraid now.

Tarron rose, striding toward me.

I imagined myself as human, trying to direct my magic toward transforming me once more. Power sparked over me, and I began to shrink. My eye level approached Tarron's, then became a bit shorter. My feet returned to normal, as did my hands.

He ran for me and swept me up in his arms. "You did it."

"I did." Elation spread through me. "Thank you for saving my sister."

He pulled back and nodded. "Of course."

I pressed a kiss to his lips, savoring the moment, then hurried to Aeri and knelt by her side.

She lunged up and hugged me. "Good job, sis. I knew you could do it."

"Right in the nick of time." I pulled back. "Are you all right?"

She nodded, then climbed slowly to her feet. I helped her, with Declan hovering by.

"How'd you do it?" Aeri asked.

"I remembered who I was." It was both as simple as that and as terribly complicated, since it'd taken me so long to figure it out.

I turned toward the army that walked toward us, searching for my friends.

Cass, Nix, and Del walked alongside Connor and Claire. All looked like hell—burned and cut, with tired eyes and pale skin. Brielle staggered along next to them, alive but wounded.

"I'm going to go help them," Tarron said. "I imagine that Brielle sent the other healers to her troops."

He loped off toward them, and I followed. Aeri and I

leaned against each other as we walked, falling naturally into sync.

"Did we really do it?" Aeri asked.

I looked toward the jubilant—and still angry—crowd of Unseelie Fae in the sky. The false queen was *definitely* gone.

"We really did it."

The coronation of the Unseelie Queen was nothing like I'd expected. For one, it was far less formal. Yet somehow even more beautiful.

Once the Unseelie Kingdom had healed its wounded and recovered from the battle, they'd set about arranging the coronation immediately. Even though they'd agreed to a democracy, I would still be queen in name and status.

A bit like the British. All the glamour without so many important decisions.

It was perfect for me. I had a life to be living, after all, and learning bureaucracy was not high on my to-do list.

Which led to me standing there, in the middle of the forest with faerie lights glittering overhead. Birds sang in the trees, and hundreds of Unseelie gathered around as the crown was placed on my head.

Tarron stood to the right, along with Aeri, Declan, and the FireSouls. Claire and Connor stood next to them. Even Aethelred had come. Everyone shot me a grin, and it was all I could do to maintain a serious face.

Despite my levity and the joy that surged through me, this *was* a serious occasion. The monarchy and its magic were still immensely important to the Unseelie Fae. The hundreds of people who'd turned up for this ceremony were proof of that.

I drew in a deep breath and met Brielle's gaze. I'd chosen her to bear the crown, and she walked across the clearing, her gaze on mine. A gown of sage green trailed behind her, and she looked amazing when she was dressed up in the ornate Fae style.

She stopped in front of me, a gorgeous silver and gold crown in her hands.

She bowed low, handing me the crown. "To the true ruler of the Unseelie Fae. Our liberator and queen."

My heart tightened as I accepted the crown and placed it upon my head. I'd had to redo my bouffant a bit for this, but the crown fit.

The entire crowd roared, cheers sending the birds toward the sky. We'd lost a record few people in the battle —both Seelie and Unseelie—and everyone was joyous.

The ceremony turned quickly into a party, with drinks and music flowing freely and loudly.

I hugged Brielle, who finally broke into a real, genuine smile. I was pretty sure she was going to end up the true democratic ruler of the Unseelie.

I pulled back and smiled at her. "I'm glad it was you."

"I'm glad it was you." Her expression turned serious. "Without you—and the dragon that lives within you—we never would have been free."

I pressed my lips together, my eyes pricking with tears. "Thank you."

Brielle squeezed my arms. "Your friends are converging on you."

I hugged her one last time, then turned to the crowd. The FireSouls were the first to hug me, and I gave each one a long look. "We've known each other a long time. I can't say that I saw this coming. But it did. And thanks—from the bottom of my heart—for the help. We couldn't have done it without you."

The three of them nodded.

"You make an amazing queen," Cass said.

"The crown is badass," Del added.

"We should get drinks sometime." Nix grinned. "I don't know many queens."

I grinned at her. "Potions & Pastilles?"

She nodded. "Potions & Pastilles."

Claire and Connor hugged me next.

"*Definitely* badass." Claire nodded toward my crown.

"You always had it in you," Connor said.

"I could get used to this kind of praise."

"Don't," Aeri said. "Because when you come home, it's life as normal."

I hugged her tight. "I wouldn't wish for anything else."

I pulled back from Aeri, and Tarron tugged me toward him. "Well, you're coming with me, first."

I shot my friends a look, raising my brows, then turned to Tarron. "I'd be delighted."

We left my friends, and I waved as we went. Tarron

pulled me into a dark copse of trees, and I went willingly —*very* willingly—into his arms.

"You were amazing," he said.

"Thank you." I grinned at him. "You know, you've said this every day since the battle." It had actually been a few days—everyone had needed time to recover.

"Have you gotten sick of it?"

"Hmmmm. No." I grinned at him. "You can keep going."

"I'd be happy to keep going for the rest of our lives."

Warmth suffused me. "Really?"

"Really." He pulled me toward him. "I love you, Mari."

"I love you, Tarron."

I kissed him, and life was perfect.

THANK YOU FOR READING!

I hope you enjoyed reading this book as much as I enjoyed writing it. Reviews are *so* helpful to authors. I really appreciate all reviews, both positive and negative. If you want to leave one, you can do so at Amazon or GoodReads.

AUTHOR'S NOTE

Hey there! I hope you enjoyed *Rise of the Fae*. This was one of my favorite books yet, partially due to the fact that many of the locations were scouted on my last research trip with fellow writers, C.N. Crawford and Jenna Wolfhart (check out their books, they are great!). It helps so much to visit the places that I write about, and I hope it helps bring it to life for you too.

First, Riveaux Abbey is an amazing place located in the North York Moors in Northern England. It is a fantastic skeleton of an ancient abbey that was originally constructed in the 12th century AD. It was placed in a remote location that would allow the monks to live their ideal of an ascetic life cut off from the outside world. As with many monasteries and holy places in England, it was destroyed by Henry VIII in the 16th century when he was dissolving the monasteries to replace them with the Anglican Church. Since then, it has lain in ruin.

I took some liberties with how I described the monks and their garments and duties. And while it is true that Christianity adopted some pagan rituals to help convert pagan locals, I invented the things about Riveaux Abbey's altar. There is an extremely impressive altar-like structure in the main part of the church, but I made up everything else about it.

I can thank C.N. Crawford for mentioning the cells found within the walls of York. She explored them on a day while I went to North York Moor for inspiration. The Guy Fawkes Inn is a real place (and also supposedly the birthplace of Guy Fawkes). We stayed there, and it was a really unique property. When it came time to write this book, it was perfect. The layout is as I described, including it's close location to the massive York Minster Cathedral.

While there are crypts under the cathedral, I invented much of what you read about to suit the story.

Clifford's Tower, the round tower castle where Mari and friends appeared upon arrival in York, is located within the city walls. It is a motte and bailey style castle, meaning that a simple round tower is constructed upon a man-made hill. Generally these castles start out as wooden structures in the 11th century AD and are sometimes replaced with stone keeps later on. There's been a castle on the site since 1068, but the stone keep wasn't built until the 13th century. The genocide that I mention in the book occurred in 1190, when 150 local Jews were killed in a pogrom where the local population trapped them in the tower. Most of the Jews died by suicide to avoid falling into the hands of the mob. It's a incredibly tragic story.

In 1684, Clifford's tower suffered an explosion that damaged the castle's military defenses to the point that they became uninhabitable. After this point, the tower was turned into a jail and prison that stayed in use until 1929.

Finally, I mention The Shambles briefly in the book. This is the area of York, England with narrow winding streets and overhanging timber-framed buildings. It is the most Medieval looking street I've ever seen, and is one of the most popular parts of York. Many of the buildings date to 1350-1475, but the street was mentioned in 1086 in the Domesday Book, so it is far older. It was originally called The Great Flesh Shambles because so many butchers worked along the street. The name The Shambles likely comes from the Anglo-Saxon word *Fleshammels,* which translates to 'flesh-shelves'. The tradition continued for centuries. In 1872, there were twenty-five butcher shops located along the street. They've now been replaced with lovely shops and restaurants, though there are some meat hooks still hanging from the exteriors of the buildings.

Finally, the underground bar in Glasgow was based upon one that isn't full of supernaturals, but it was very cool and underground. The islands where the dragons live are based upon the Slate Islands, part of the Inner Hebrides off the coast of Scotland. They are truly amazing islands made of black slate that were quarried from AD 1630 until the beginning of the 20th century. Millions of tons of slate came from these smalls islands and roofed buildings all over the world. It is an incredible windswept place, perfect for Dragons.

Thank you for going on Mari's adventure with her. While her series is now complete, there will be more to come from the rest of the Magic's Bend gang.

Happy reading!

ACKNOWLEDGMENTS

Thank you, Ben, for everything. There would be no books without you.

Thank you to Jena O'Connor and Lindsey Loucks for your excellent editing. The book is immensely better because of you! Thank you to Aisha Panjwaneey for your helpful comments about typos.

Thank you to Orina Kafe for the beautiful cover art.

ABOUT LINSEY

Before becoming a writer, Linsey Hall was a nautical archaeologist who studied shipwrecks from Hawaii and the Yukon to the UK and the Mediterranean. She credits fantasy and historical romances with her love of history and her career as an archaeologist. After a decade of tromping around the globe in search of old bits of stuff that people left lying about, she settled down and started penning her own romance novels. Her Dragon's Gift series draws upon her love of history and the paranormal elements that she can't help but include.

COPYRIGHT

CPSIA information can be obtained
at www.ICGtesting.com
Printed in the USA
LVHW091754041219
639425LV00002B/323/P